BLING-BLING, YOU'RE DEAD!

When the manager of newly-formed girl band Bling-Bling needs a Surveillance Operator to protect them, retired policeman Bill Muir jumps at the chance — but he doesn't know what he's let himself in for . . . In *Making Changes*, Tania Harkness is on a mission to turn around her run-down estate. But someone else is equally determined to stop her . . . And in *Another Country*, Shona Graham returns to her native Orkney island of Hundsay to put right a wrong that saw her brother ostracised by the community many years previously . . .

GERALDINE RYAN

BLING-BLING, YOU'RE DEAD!
& Other Stories

Complete and Unabridged

LINFORD
Leicester

First published in Great Britain

This Linford Edition
published 2016

A catalogue record for this book is available
from the British Library.

ISBN 978–1–4448–3096–5

Contents

Bling-Bling, You're Dead!

Bill Muir's retirement was short-lived. It lasted four weeks and three days, to be precise, though he'd started to feel like a hen on a hot griddle even before his first week was up.

During those first seven days, he pondered the idea of making a few phone calls to some of his old mates in the Force to see if they knew of anybody who might be looking for somebody with his experience of detection.

It was an idea he abandoned almost immediately, knowing just how easily such a course of action might be misconstrued. In no time at all, word would get round down the station that he wasn't coping very well since he'd handed in his badge. It was a fair point — he wasn't — but he had his pride.

At the start of week two, he took to dragging the dog for a walk, and leaving Rex to loiter forlornly outside the library while he went inside and checked the Sits Vac in the online edition of the local paper. He didn't like leaving the poor creature out there, at the mercy of the elements and old ladies with shopping trolleys who thought nothing of blithely running their wheels over whichever part of a waiting dog's anatomy happened to get in their way.

But needs must. There was Pam, his wife of thirty years and mother of his two children, to consider. If she found out what he was up to, she'd go mad. Even before the date of his retirement had been officially confirmed, she'd been on Facebook to Joely in Sydney chatting about getting a flight over to see the grandchildren.

He should have said something then. But while he'd still been busy working, it was just too easy to convince himself that his retirement was but a dot on the landscape. Of course, he longed to see Joely and the grandchildren as much as Pam did. But Pam was talking about staying four or five weeks. What did a man do with himself in a place like Australia for a month if he didn't like cricket or heat and couldn't stand barbecues? But still he continued to say nothing and felt bad.

The call came out of the blue when he'd been home three weeks. It was his old mate and fellow Detective Constable Jack Devlin on the phone.

'Maggie Quinn. Manages pop stars. I heard on the grapevine she's looking for someone to do a job. Sounds right up your street,' Devlin said, once the preliminaries were over.

Bill pricked up his ears. 'Sounds interesting,' he said.

'From what I can gather it sounds like she's after someone to do a bit of surveillance. Interested?'

Bill Muir was a copper to his very marrow. A man with no hobbies and no wanderlust who was too old to change. The thought of one more shopping expedition to John Lewis, trailing round after Pam while she stroked socks or asked his opinion on the design of a tea towel, was more than this one man could bear. Australia drifted away into the deep blue yonder.

'I might end up regretting saying this,' he sighed. 'But, yes. I am.'

'A job?'

Pam was in the middle of peeling her soggy swimming things away from the plastic bag she always kept them in and cramming them into the drum.

'I thought it would give me something to do.'

'There's plenty to do round here.'

He'd walked into that one.

'And what about Australia?' She peered up at him from her position squatting on the kitchen floor, her eyes glinting from behind her specs.

'Pam . . . ' He made a consolatory gesture with his arm. 'About that . . . '

Pam slammed the door of the washing machine shut, set the dial and pressed Start.

'You had no intention of going to Australia, did you?' she demanded. 'You've just been humouring me.'

'We can go another time,' he said lamely, hating himself for being such a coward.

'*You* can,' she replied, scrambling to

her feet. 'My ticket's booked already. I'm leaving in five days.'

And with that bombshell, she headed for the door.

★   ★   ★

On the phone, Maggie Quinn had told him that she suspected someone of trying to sabotage the success of Bling-Bling, the new girl band she was about to launch on tour. Two questions presented themselves immediately to Bill. What, exactly, did she mean by *sabotage*; and why didn't she call the police if she was so concerned? She answered them in reverse order.

'This launch has been planned for months,' she said. 'I've invested energy, time and money in it. I can't risk the police telling me to postpone it while they poke about trying to discover whoever it is who is trying to harm my girls.'

'Harm them?'

Maggie Quinn lowered her voice. Bill made a stab at guessing what she looked like. Motherly, from her use of the term *my girls*, he decided.

'There's been stuff,' she said. 'Last week, during rehearsals, the pyrotechnics misfired. It was a real explosion. Singed Leila's eyebrows right off. Then, later in the day, there was an incident with the dry ice.'

'In what way?'

'There was far too much of it. I couldn't make any of them out from the third row of the stalls. Poor girls ended up coughing and spluttering so much they couldn't sing a note; and Inez had such a bad asthma attack, we had to get the paramedics in.'

'Accidents, though, surely?' Bill said.

'Maybe. But how do you explain ground glass in the costumes?'

Bill couldn't.

'And then there's this other thing which makes me think someone's got it in for them. Two days ago, the girls rang me up hysterical,' she said. 'When I went along to the theatre, they took me round to the dressing-room. Someone had daubed some words on a mirror in lipstick.'

'What words?' Bill wanted to know.

' '*Bling-Bling, you're dead*',' said Maggie Quinn, after a dramatic pause.

★ ★ ★

Bill was doing his homework, guiltily Googling images and information on *Bling-Bling*, while above his head the floorboards of the marital bedroom creaked beneath Pam's feet as she flitted between wardrobe, chest of drawers and suitcase, packing for her trip.

Doing his best to ignore it, he clicked on an image of five scantily dressed young women with big hair — and the kind of breasts that come with a receipt, a guarantee and a how-to-care-for booklet — posing for the camera. Several more photos showed them up on stage, strutting their stuff while bronzed male dancers exhibited their — er — finer points.

Underneath the make-up, the hair extensions and the fake tans he felt sure there must be four pretty girls hiding somewhere. He thought of *his* girls, Joely and Hilly, and felt suddenly sad at how quickly time had flown. They were women now, both of them, with frown lines and responsibilities. But, even as girls, they'd never looked as glamorous as these four. Quietly, he thanked God for it. If they had, he'd never have got a night's sleep.

His mobile rang. It was Maggie Quinn.

'So, Bill, made up your mind yet?'

The memory of his last conversation with Pam replayed in his head. He would have gone with her to Australia, he'd told her. But not yet. He just needed a bit more time to get used to the idea. Pam had brushed his words away. Life was for living, she'd told him. Not for thinking about. And then she'd gone and ordered her taxi. This time tomorrow, she'd be up in the air. So, all in all, what did he have to lose in agreeing to accompany Bling-Bling on tour in the role of Surveillance Operator? Which was the fancy name Maggie Quinn had come up with for a bloke charged with keeping his eyes and ears open.

'Yes,' he found himself saying. 'I am.'

'Good. First thing we must do is introduce you to the girls.'

'I've already met them — in a sort of a way,' he said. 'I'm just Googling their images.'

'Really?' She seemed pleased to hear it. 'And what do you think?'

'Very nice,' he said, omitting to add, *If you like that sort of thing.*

'This time next year, Bling-Bling will be more popular than Little Mix.' She sounded just like a proud mother, he thought; until she added, 'So you see how important it is, don't you, Bill, that nothing goes wrong and spoils my plans for them?'

For a moment there, she'd almost managed to fool him. Not quite, though. Maggie Quinn was an empire-builder. That wasn't motherly pride he'd heard just then in her steely voice. It was sheer ambitious greed.

'They're performing live to a TV audience tomorrow,' she continued. 'It'll be an opportunity for you to meet them, and hear exactly what they have to say about what's been happening recently. Unless you already have plans,' she added.

Pam would be on a plane this time tomorrow. The house would be empty apart from the dog. Maybe he'd take Rex down to The Man in the Moon for a pie and a pint. Did that count as a plan?

Oh, what the hell. The only way he and Pam could patch things up now was if one of them backed down completely, and that was never going to happen. Not while she felt so angry and he felt so manipulated.

'I look forward to meeting them,' he said.

* * *

Bill's heart had plummeted when he'd learned that the daytime show Bling-Bling would be performing in was none other than *ChickChat*. It was one of those dreadful programmes — of which there were many — that Pam was addicted to.

Four women shouting over each other and poking fun at men. *If it was the other way round, the programme would have been taken off the air years ago,* he'd commented after one particular gruelling tirade about his gender.

It is the other way round for most of the time, Pam had replied, without taking her eyes off the screen. *You only have to pick up a newspaper or switch on the TV and you'll see some poor woman being castigated for failing to fall in with society's views of how she should live her life. Least you can do is give us one measly hour a day to get our own back.* Then she'd turned up the volume, putting an end to any further discussion. Had she always been such a feminist?

Now, the morning after their phone call, Maggie Quinn, who'd met him at the TV studios, greeted him in her usual brusque manner. Having been waved through by security, they were now on their way to the Green Room — where, so Maggie said, the girls would be whiling away the time before the show began.

'*ChickChat*'s not everyone's cup of tea, but it'll be a great gig for the girls as they'll be on for the whole hour; plus, they'll get to perform their new single at the end of the show. And viewing figures are huge too,' she said.

13

Bill could almost see the flashing pound signs in her eyes as she spoke. He decided to concentrate on the route they were taking. There were CCTV cameras everywhere, and all of the areas they passed had entrances that could only be accessed by some sort of code, which cheered him somewhat. If there was some loony nursing bad intentions towards Bling-Bling, then they were going to have to overcome an awful lot of obstacles before they made it inside, he decided.

The walls were lined with blown-up photos and handprints of famous stars of the small screen, all signed. He'd never been one of those who'd gone gaga whenever he'd spotted a celebrity, although he'd make an exception for Felicity Kendall. Pam, a real celebrity spotter, would be thrilled when he described it to her, though. Then he remembered — Pam wasn't at home.

True to her word, she'd got in her taxi and driven away. *Don't bother seeing me off*, she'd told him the night before. *I'm leaving early.* In the event, he had got up. But only to stand by the bedroom window and watch the taxi pull away. Perhaps even then he hadn't believed she'd go through with it. But she'd proved him wrong.

'Right. Brace yourself. When all four of them are together, they can sometimes be a force to be reckoned with.'

Maggie Quinn yanked him back to the here and now as, with a curt nod to the runner who scurried to open the door for them, she led the way into the Green Room. Bill stood around like a spare part while Maggie greeted her girls. There was much squealing and air-kissing, mixed in with a clash of voices as the girls fought for Maggie's attention with a list of demands, complaints and observations.

His first impression was that they didn't look much like they had in the photo Maggie Quinn had shown him. Their publicity shots had shown them as fierce in their heavy make-up and revealing costumes; whereas here, casually dressed and only lightly made-up, while they were all undoubtedly pretty girls, only Leila, in his eyes, could have been considered a beauty. Not that he would ever think of judging any woman on her physical attributes alone, of course.

Bill took the opportunity to observe them in turn. From their official website, he'd gleaned the following information about their personalities. Flame-haired Neela was Irish and bubbly, and had a way with animals. Bea was Welsh, bilingual, and with a great sense of humour.

Blonde Ginny was 'the quiet one'; Inez had Mexican blood and a fiery temper; and Leila, whose parents ran an Indian takeaway that was very popular among the students of Leicester, had learned to make chapattis at her mother's knee and cooked for the girls whenever she could.

'Who's this, then?'

Bea was the first to spot him. Short, with intelligent eyes set in a small, square-jawed face, the look she gave him could only have been described as antagonistic.

'This is Bill,' said Maggie. 'He's our new Surveillance Officer. He'll be touring with us, and generally keeping an eye on you girls.'

Five pairs of eyes were fixed on him

now. One pair of amber, a sparkling pair of green, two pairs of deepest brown, and a suspicious pair of blue.

Those were the ones he addressed first. 'Ginny, isn't it?' he asked. 'Maggie tells me you found ground glass in one of your tops.'

Tossing her platinum locks, she stared at him defiantly. 'Are you police?' she demanded.

Being Police was obviously a Bad Thing. Better to hedge, he decided.

'Not any more,' he said. 'Like Maggie said, I'm a surveillance officer. I'll be coming with you on tour, generally keeping an eye out for your safety and hopefully deterring any further attempts at sabotage.'

'Get him. Has he swallowed a dictionary?'

The girls burst into peals of laughter. Bea's Cardiff accent sliced right through him. What was her problem with him? He turned to speak to her.

'It must have been very distressing for you when you discovered those words daubed on the mirror the other week,' he said in his best sympathetic manner.

'I'll live,' she sneered. 'But, like Ginny said, we don't need no police snooping round. We're perfectly capable of fighting our own battles, thanks very much.'

'Bea grew up on a very rough estate,' Maggie explained, almost apologetically. 'She's not always well-disposed to the law, even when they're ex-law.'

'That's 'cause they've never given me no reason to like them,' Bea said.

There was an uncomfortable silence. It was Inez who filled it in the end.

'I'm sure we'll all feel a bit safer if we know someone's looking out for us,' she said. 'After the incident with the dry ice that set my asthma off, I'm really worried it'll happen again.'

Immediately, Neela and Leila were at her side, murmuring reassuringly. Bea, for her part, remained where she was.

'It won't, Inez,' she said, raising her eyes heavenward. 'How many more times do we have to tell you?'

'I know, I'm sorry,' Inez said. 'I'm sure you're right.'

'For the next three weeks while you're on tour,' Maggie said, 'you just concentrate on getting your performance pitch-perfect, right? There are still plenty of things which need ironing out.'

Inez nodded.

'Leave everything else to Bill, myself, and the rest of the team, who are all here to look after you.'

'Apart from the eejit who's after killing us all!' Flame-haired Neela spoke for the first time. He got the impression she didn't feel remotely threatened, personally. Ah, what it was to be young and feel invincible.

'Five minutes please, girls!'

A second runner appeared, complete with clipboard and earpiece.

'Mr Muir, you need to take your seat in the studio audience now,' she said. 'My colleague will escort you. She's waiting for you outside this room.'

'Thanks,' he said. 'Good luck, girls,' he added.

But none of them were looking his way. They were all too busy staring in the mirrors, making a few last-minute adjustments to their make-up.

The set had been divided into two halves, boasting very different styles. One half looked like a show-house living room. There was a lot of beige and a great deal of pink, lending a very feminine feel.

The other half of the stage was set up for a musical performance. The rigging that overarched this part of the set made for a much edgier atmosphere, with angled lights and dangling ropes that gave the appearance of urban scaffolding.

He was brought back to reality as the panel walked on and took their seats to rapturous applause. Then, after a brief and banal discussion of the day's news, Bling-Bling walked on to even greater applause.

The girls displayed none of the animosity they'd shown him when it came to chatting to the panel of presenters. Quite the opposite, in fact — all were sweetness and light. Bill, never one for bearing a grudge, resolved to put any previous tetchiness down to stage fright.

After the break, there was a change of

mood as Bling-Bling, singing a track from their new album — *Give Me Your Word* — were welcomed back onstage. The auditorium darkened so that only the silhouettes of the girls were immediately visible.

Gradually, their dramatically-made-up faces came into focus as they began to lip-synch. There was a great deal of gyrating and not a small amount of exposed flesh; and the audience, as far as Bill could tell, was loving it.

Their performance was very nearly at an end when Bill's attention was suddenly drawn upwards towards the rigging, from where an odd creaking sound had begun to intrude into his enjoyment of the song.

It looked very much as if one of the lamps had worked itself loose and was now swinging dangerously out of control. Worked itself loose — or been tampered with? Bill sat forward in his seat, poised to act. Something was about to go badly wrong for Bling-Bling, he was sure of it. As the heavy light with its sharp metal edges began to descend, people in the audience screamed, while others stood in their seats and watched in silent horror.

Bill was sitting on the second row. He was no athlete, but his copper's reflexes propelled him forward. Clambering over the seat in front of him, he dashed forward onto the stage.

Without a second thought, Bill lunged at the girls, scattering them squealing to all four corners of the set. Then a roar went up from the crowd and the whole place was plunged into darkness.

* * *

Bill wished they'd all stop discussing him as if he wasn't there. So what if he *had* turned a small hand towel bright red, and slid off a chair onto the floor?! *Chick-Chat*'s hosts, he recognised, but all these other people seemed to have materialised from nowhere. An army of women — some in suits and stilettos, others in jeans and trainers — all talking over each other and waving clipboards, rushing around like maniacs.

Only the girls, moving in and out of his hazy eyeline and arguably the cause of his accident, remained remote from the mayhem. Fortunately, the audience appeared to have been sent home. Otherwise they'd have doubtless joined the party too, adding their voices to the clamour up here on the stage.

A number of various diagnoses had already been reached by the assembled throng. It was as if they were taking part in an auction, determined to outbid each other on the seriousness of his injuries. *I'll bid concussion! I'll see your concussion and raise you delayed shock!*

It was all nonsense, of course. Didn't they know he was an ex-police officer, a man who'd been thumped more times than Frank Bruno? A single glancing blow from a hot stage light, albeit one in freefall and with jagged metal edges, was nothing to someone who'd spent more Saturday afternoons in the thick of it down at Millwall FC's home ground than he cared to remember.

'Clear a space, please. Stretcher coming through.'

Men. At last. Two of them. He could see their sturdy flat feet approaching, sending stilettos and trainers scattering.

They'd been serious about the ambulance, then. Honestly, he didn't know where to put himself. If only his mates could see him now. He'd be a laughing stock.

* * *

Bill came out of the treatment room sporting one of those invisible plasters on his forehead but otherwise pronounced fit to go, bearing in mind the usual warnings about coming back if he developed any worsening symptoms.

Just in case he was in any doubt about the exact nature of these symptoms, the nurse who'd fixed him up had presented him with a leaflet, which she said would explain what they were. He was reading this in the lobby, waiting for the taxi to take him home, when Maggie Quinn swept in.

'Bill! There you are!'

She marched over to him. After fastidiously examining the seat next to his, she sat down on it.

'How *are* you?'

Swiftly closing the distance he'd opened

up between them as she leaned in towards him, she squinted at his forehead. Her features softened as she made the kind of soppy noises Pam was prone to indulge in whenever she saw one of the grand-children fast asleep in a cosy babygro or cutely packaged in a towel at bath time.

'It's nothing, honestly,' he said.

'No, it's not nothing, Bill. I've seen the footage. You may well have saved one of those girls a nasty cut on the head.'

'Anyone would have done the same,' he insisted.

'Well, there was absolutely no evidence of that on the tape I saw. There was only *one* man who risked his own safety to save those young girls, and that was you, Bill.'

Bill had once won a medal for disarming a desperate man intent on wiping out his entire family. But for the life of him, he wouldn't have known where to lay his hands on it if anyone should ask to see it. And if ever Pam brought up the subject of his officially recognised bravery when they had friends round, he always used it as an opportunity to pop into the kitchen for a bit of a clear-up.

Pam. He couldn't seem to get her out of his mind. How long did it take to fly to Sydney, exactly? Would she call him when she arrived, or at the very least email him? Or had she decided to maintain the silence between them for as long as it took for him to see sense (or what passed as her version of it)?

'Anyway, what are you doing sitting here still? Haven't they finished with you yet?'

Maggie Quinn's words cut into his thoughts. He was waiting for a taxi, he told her. She waved that idea away immediately. She had her car outside with the engine still running. Her driver would take him anywhere he wanted to go.

'Home would be nice,' he said, wistfully.

'Then home it is, Bill. We can talk there.'

There was nothing for it but to accept her offer, he realised; not without some trepidation.

'Right,' she said, jumping up from her seat. 'Let's get out of here before we both get struck down by some dreadful infection.'

★　★　★

Maggie Quinn was making tea for both of them in Bill's kitchen while he sat and watched. The thought of what Pam would say if she were to walk in and discover another woman riffling through her tea-bags and making free with her semi-skimmed milk made him feel uneasy.

When it was ready, she set it down in front of him and took the seat opposite, sending out waves of such strong perfume they almost sent Bill reeling. When had she had the opportunity to spray herself with that little lot? he wondered. More worryingly, why?

It occurred to him that her Roller was parked right outside his front door, complete with uniformed chauffeur, and he was certain he'd spotted curtains twitching as they'd got out and walked into the house together.

It would be all round the neighbour-hood before long that he'd lost no opportunity to install his fancy woman as soon as Pam's back was turned, even though there was no truth in it.

'Nice house, this,' Maggie Quinn piped up. 'Your wife out at work, is she?'

Was it that obvious that he was a married man? Bill wondered. His glance fell on the coaster he'd slipped beneath his mug so as not to make a mark, seconds before Maggie Quinn had set it down. Only a domesticated man would have such an automatic reaction to an approaching mug of hot liquid.

He decided to stick to the basic facts. She'd gone to Australia — that very morning, actually. She'd be away a good few weeks, visiting their daughter and the grandchildren.

'I really ought to ring her,' he added randomly, forgetting for a second that she was probably still on the plane.

'So, you're on your own just now, then?' Widening her eyes, she gazed at him over her mug. 'Just like me.'

Pam had often told him he was a bit slow on the uptake where women were concerned. But he'd got the message now all right. He smiled weakly. Then, from some dark recess of Maggie Quinn's handbag, the sinister theme music of *Kill Bill* suddenly erupted. He was flooded with the kind of relief he imagined a man

28

in the dock might feel, one who'd just received a *Not guilty* verdict.

'You'd better not let that ring,' he said. 'You never know, it might be important.'

She hesitated, but only for a moment. Thankfully for Bill, Maggie Quinn was a woman for whom business would always come before pleasure.

The conversation was brief. Maggie barely appeared to be listening, but when the call came to an end, she quickly demonstrated that she'd taken everything she needed to know.

'That was the studio floor manager,' she said.

Bill pricked up his ears. 'Did he say if they thought what happened was an accident or deliberate?'

He cursed the fact that he was no longer a serving detective. He had no authority to order a search of the set. Neither could he go marching in demanding to inter-view everyone who had access to that particular area. He was a mere surveil-lance manager, a trumped-up title for a trumped-up job — a security guard by another name.

She shrugged. 'Oh, that,' she said. 'I didn't ask him.'

Her lips curled in a self-satisfied smile as she stared into the distance. She had the look of a woman forming a plan.

'If one of the girls had received a cut on the face or a bruise back there, it would have looked very bad for the TV studios,' she said, picking out her words with slow deliberation.

Bill stared at her, at a loss to understand the turn in the conversation.

'Grovelling, he was. Quite sweet, really. Obviously expects a lawsuit slapped on him.' Delight shone in her eyes at this unexpected turn of events.

Bill felt suddenly dismayed. If he'd suspected it before, now he was certain. Money lay at the heart of everything that motivated her, he realised. If she stood to make more from a claim for damages than from finding out who was attempting to sabotage the girls' tour, then it was a no-brainer that she'd choose to pursue the former.

He felt a sudden fervent wish that he could tell her he'd changed his mind about working for her. But it was out of the question. He's signed a contract now. Tomorrow morning at nine o'clock he'd be on that tour bus heading for Newcastle, their first stop. Maggie Quinn had him over the proverbial barrel.

But if he couldn't get out of it, then he'd do the job to the best of his ability. If she wanted a surveillance manager, then that's exactly what she'd get. He'd get to the bottom of this mystery if it were the last thing he did.

★   ★   ★

The girl crept into the dressing-room and surveyed it in rapturous awe. *Be quick,* her brother had told her. *You've got five minutes, that's all.* She hadn't argued, afraid that any objection she might make — that five minutes was nowhere near long enough, for example — would only serve to make him change his mind. He was risking his job letting her inside, and the last thing she wanted was to get him into trouble.

Oh, it was absolutely amazing in here!

So many beautiful things contained in one room. Clothes, accessories, and a bewildering display of brushes and make-up. Spotting the dresses she guessed they'd worn for their opening number, she edged towards them, and scrunched some of the material in her hand.

Glimpsing a sudden movement in the mirror, she jumped, thrown into a panic, until she realised that what she saw was her own reflection. She took a few deep breaths to calm herself down, inhaling the heady mix of different perfumes that lingered still on the warm air, even though Bling-Bling had left for the stage a good fifteen minutes previously.

Cautiously, she crept towards the nearest dressing table. *Five minutes.* That was all she had. Less now. What she'd have really liked would be to grab a souvenir and run off with it. But one of the girls might miss it. She might be accused of theft, and her brother would be sacked immediately.

What if she simply tried out some of the girls' make-up? She tugged at one of the drawers, and a box marked *Samples* jumped out at her. Perfect! Riffling through, she selected a small palette. Eyeshadow. *Hot spice*. Hard to tell the shade — she didn't dare risk discovery by switching on more lights. But Bling-Bling were always made up to perfection, so whatever the colour, she knew the result would be excellent.

With trembling hand she opened the box and, reaching for a small brush, hurriedly began to apply the shadow, first to one eyelid and then the next. There. Done. She blinked. Even before she'd dropped the brush, her lids began to burn and her eyes started to smart. She rubbed at them with increasing urgency, but that only made things worse. Now her knuckles were burning too!

It was as if her eyeballs had been run through with a corkscrew. She needed to get out of here. Blindly, she fumbled her way towards the door, letting out a loud wail of pain, no longer caring who heard her. Her sobs brought the sound of running feet, the door burst open, and before she knew it she'd fallen right into someone's arms. They belonged to a man — big, strong, reassuring. Hysterically, she began to scream.

'You're okay,' he said. 'I've got you. You'll be fine.'

'Help!' she cried. 'You've got to help me! I've been blinded!'

★ ★ ★

Bling-Bling were still in full make-up and the costumes they'd worn for the finale. Everyone was talking at once.

'Chilli powder in the eye shadow?'

'But how did it get in our dressing-room?'

'And what about the girl! How did *she* get in?'

A harmony of *Right! Good question!*

'Aren't you supposed to be in charge of surveillance, Bill? How did you let that one slip by?'

A synchronicity of outraged *Yeah*s. And *Explain that, then*s.

'Who was she, did they say? The sister of one of the theatre staff?'

'So she's the one who's been causing all this trouble! I hope they've got her locked up!'

A verse of agreement at this remark, accompanied by a veritable chorus of frantic nods and arm-waving.

Bill waited for the fire that was Bling-Bling to blow itself out. He was used to girls. This was what they did. Asked questions — then, instead of waiting for the answers, blindly cast around for some that best suited their own mad theories. It was much more fun that way, and if they could do one of their own sex down into the bargain, so much the better. He'd had enough. Holding up his hands for silence — which was a long time coming — he finally spoke.

'Actually, no, they haven't got her locked up. They've got her in A&E still, poor girl.'

That put out their fire. Even the Welsh dragon's — Bea's. It would have been nice, he said, if they'd expressed some concern for the victim. She was a fan of theirs, and they should be flattered by just how badly she'd wanted to get a glimpse of their dressing-room. Which was how she'd explained her reasons for being there to Bill, who'd accompanied her to the hospital and stayed with her, holding her hand throughout, while a nurse washed her poor eyes.

'It was all she wanted. To see where you all hung out backstage. She's a nice, loyal girl. Attaches no blame to her brother, who's part of the crew. Says he tried to discourage her, but she refused to let it drop. And, in case you need reminding — which, in fact, I think you do — you owe her a big thank-you,' he added. 'Any one of you five could have applied that eyeshadow and been where she is now.'

'Hear, hear!'

Everyone spun round. There was Maggie Quinn, newly arrived from London where she'd been attending a raft of meetings before flying up to Newcastle on a friend's private aircraft to catch the girls' stage debut.

'I hope you're all suitably chastened,' she said, twinkling her eyes at Bill.

'Yeah, but . . . ' Bea said, casting her eyes downward.

'We're sorry for her, course,' Ginny butted in. 'But you can't expect us to feel safe now after this.'

'Ginny's right,' Leila said. 'That girl could have been blinded. More importantly, one of us could have been.'

The girls nodded in fervent agreement. Bill boggled at what he'd just heard Leila say. What would they be like with a number one under their belt, he wondered, if they were so full of themselves even before the reviews of their first live concert were out?

'Well, the important thing is that none of you were,' Maggie snapped back, in her no-nonsense manner. Turning to Bill, her tone grew soft. 'That's why Bill's here, remember,' she said. 'To keep an eye out for you.'

Bea and Neela nudged each other and sniggered at Maggie's unfortunate turn of phrase. Maggie glared at them. When they glared back, defiantly, Maggie appeared taken aback for a split-second, but quickly recovered herself.

'And he's done it very well so far,' she said. 'But what we need now is a good bit of PR. We can make headlines with this. A visit to the girl's home. Flowers. Tickets to the show. Magnanimity towards her prat of a brother who should be fired for letting her in.'

She was on a roll now. Bill allowed her words to wash over him. He was busy watching the girls. They weren't exactly sharing Maggie's delight at the way things had turned out tonight. In fact, the atmosphere was bordering on the mutinous.

But by the next day their sour mood had completely evaporated and they were graciousness personified. The PR visit went splendidly by all accounts, the poor unfortunate victim satisfied with Maggie's waffley explanation that the chilli incident was just a silly prank.

Bill was far from satisfied, however. Taking Maggie to one side, he'd pleaded with her to allow the police to investigate the incident. But, just as he'd predicted, she'd refused. They had six more performances left, she reminded him. If he could just keep the ship afloat till then, she'd consider it.

He'd longed to discuss what theories, if any, she had about who might have been responsible. A jealous dancer, perhaps; or one of the make-up girls who'd taken a dislike to any of the singers? But, as usual, her phone rang just as he was about to broach the subject, and he was dismissed.

Now Bling-Bling were back on stage in front of a new audience for the second time in as many days. The girls had done three up-tempo numbers before the lighting dimmed and the mood altered. They struck a pose, and the audience held their breath, and waited for the music intro to the next song. And waited . . . and waited . . . and waited.

From the wings, Bill couldn't see the audience. But he sensed their increasing restiveness. When it became clear to the girls that no music was coming, they began to search around for some support, bewilderment and growing panic on their faces.

He hoped they weren't trying to catch *his* eye! He wouldn't have had a clue how to fix their expensive equipment. He'd once bought himself an iPod when thinking he might take up jogging. Initially, Joely had put all the music on it for him, because he'd no idea how to do it himself. That had been five years ago, and he was still stuck with the same playlist now. He'd got so sick of hearing the same tunes that in the end he'd had to give up jogging altogether.

Inez, who appeared to have been appointed spokesperson, finally addressed the audience. 'Looks like something's happened to the music system, guys!' she said, trying to make light of the situation.

The audience began to vent their disapproval. Inez held up her hand to silence them.

'We've agreed we're going to do this next song a *cappella*.' She glanced towards her fellow group members for support. 'Isn't that right, girls?'

There was some discussion — at one point it looked as if Bea, at least, wasn't up for that — but the clamouring audience finally decided it. Bill felt a movement at his side. It was Maggie, almost apoplectic with rage.

'Someone's fixing it!' she hissed. 'I've told them to pull the ruddy curtain down till it's done. Does no one listen to a word I say?'

Apparently not, Bill mused. He got the impression that Maggie didn't think much of their chances of pulling this off. Something to do with the way she hid her eyes behind her hands. What she said next was a big clue, too.

'If those girls start singing without any music, it will expose them. The fans will be brutal. This is going to finish them before they've got properly started.'

And then the girls opened their mouths to sing.

⋆ ⋆ ⋆

Bill had been vaguely aware of Maggie's grip on his arm within seconds of the girls beginning. But then he'd surrendered himself to the sweet sound of their harmony and become totally oblivious to everything else. Now the song had ended, she turned to him, tears welling in her eyes.

'But that was beautiful,' she croaked, as if it was the last thing in the world she'd expected.

The audience, equally affected by

Bling-Bling's *a cappella* performance, had risen to their feet in rapturous applause. It went on for a long time while Bling-Bling jumped up and down in delight, hugging each other and blowing ecstatic kisses to the audience. Then the music caught them all quite unawares as, finally and miraculously restored, it suddenly struck up again, catapulting them into their next song.

'Well,' Maggie said, 'I might have harboured a few doubts about Bling-Bling's singing ability before now. But not any more.'

Ah, this was more like the hard-bitten Maggie Quinn Bill recognised.

'We'll have to do more to bring Inez and Neela to the fore,' she went on. 'Those two have definitely got the best voices. And Leila has the looks, of course. It'll be interesting to see if there are any reviews of tonight's performance in the papers tomorrow, don't you think?'

Bill was having some difficulty making out everything she said over the music. He cupped his ear with his hand to let her know as much. 'Look, can we go somewhere quieter?'

'There's always my room,' she replied.

Bill thought fast. Best thing was to pretend he hadn't heard what she'd said, he decided.

'Just come a bit further away from all this noise,' he said. 'I can't hear a word you say.'

Maggie Quinn was as determined a lady in her personal life as she was in her professional one, he concluded. He'd managed to avoid her clutches this time. *But for how much longer?* he wondered, as together they moved deeper into the wings.

★   ★   ★

Next day everyone piled back on the bus for the next leg of their tour. Bill had imagined that after last night's triumph, the girls would still be on the top of the world. But instead, their mood this morning was tetchy.

Bea, who was particularly grumpy, took up two seats and lay sprawled out over both of them, listening to her iPod with her eyes shut. Neela sat behind her in the window seat, staring outside, studiously avoiding conversation and eye contact with Inez in the seat next to hers, who was playing with her phone and equally studiously avoiding Neela. Leila appeared to be asleep, and Ginny had her head buried in a magazine, furiously chewing gum.

He wandered over from his seat to where Maggie Quinn was immersed in something she was reading on her laptop screen. He wanted to ask her something. In the seat next to her was a pile of well-thumbed newspapers.

'Move them if you want to sit down,' she said, not taking her eyes off the screen.

He did as she asked. The top newspaper was open at the music page. The headlines jumped out at him: *Bling-Bling Can Sing-Sing*, he read. *Was that the best they could come up with?* he wondered, before reading on.

This particular reviewer had hitherto been of the opinion hitherto the UK didn't need another averagely talented bland girl band. But, after watching them perform at Newcastle's City Hall last night, a mess-up with the backing music system had revealed that at least two of the girls had very fine voices indeed, Bill read.

He skimmed the rest of the review before making his way through the other papers, all of which were open at reviews dedicated to Bling-Bling. And they were all saying the same thing.

'Have the girls fallen out?' he asked Maggie in a hushed voice.

'You've read those pieces, I take it?' she said. 'There's more of the same online. So my best guess is: yes, they very probably have.'

'Oh dear. It must make things very difficult for you when one half of the girls are being praised, and the other half criticized for simply making up the numbers.'

'Not really, Bill,' she said. 'I'll just have to manage them. That *is* my job, after all.'

Last night, Bill had begun to wonder if he'd got Maggie Quinn wrong when he'd seen how moved she was by the girls singing *a cappella*. Observing her now, though, it was as if that had never happened.

Bling-Bling's resolution to avoid each other lasted for the rest of the journey. But then later in the hotel lobby as they waited to be booked in, Bill observed the girls in a huddle, all talking at once. He moved closer in a bid to eavesdrop and managed to pick up some of what they were saying, none of it very helpful, until Bea, who was constitutionally incapable of keeping her voice low, yelled, '*Who do you two think you are?*'

She appeared to be addressing her question to Neela and Inez, who exchanged nervous glances. Ginny nodded in fervent agreement, but said nothing. Leila — the one girl whom the press had left alone, apart from commenting on her stunning beauty — looked away as if she couldn't bear to witness any more bickering, and caught his eye.

She held his gaze for a long time before she finally broke it and moved away from the girls, as if it was more than she could stand being with them any longer. It was enough to make him wonder. Was she attempting to tell him something?

Later, as he lay on his bed and rested before the girls' performance, which he would be expected to attend, he thought about the incident some more. Bea was a terrier, and she was the first to admit it.

What was it she'd told him when they first met? Something about not needing anyone to fight her battles for her, if he remembered correctly. She had a battle on her hands now, all right. To keep her place in Bling-Bling when the press agreed she was the weakest link, with Ginny not that far behind.

How far would she go to keep it? As far as terrorising the other girls with threats written in lipstick on a changing room mirror? Or planting ground glass and chilli flakes where they could have caused real harm?

Bill thought back to that first accident he'd witnessed with the lamp. If it had struck anyone, it would have been Inez and Neela who'd have copped it — the two girls with the best voices.

Was Bea the one responsible for everything that had gone wrong so far?

'Woo-hoo! Hello Leeds!' the girls shrieked, setting off a tsunami of waving and cheering in the audience. At least they had the decency to act as if they liked each other now they were onstage.

Bill checked his phone again. It was becoming an obsession. Still no message from Pam, though. She was holding out much longer over this than he'd ever expected. What did she expect him to do? Grovel?

His train of thought was suddenly interrupted by the sound of a gruff male voice. If it wasn't such an unlikely possibility he'd have sworn blind it was coming from one of the speakers.

'*Four Wheels Good*. Do you require a cab?' it went.

'Yes, please. As soon as possible. I need someone to take me to the supermarket. Can you send Charlie?' the quavering voice of an elderly lady replied.

'I'll do my best, love.' The man again.

There followed a deafening riff of interference before the gruff male voice came through again.

'Anyone in the Huntingdon Avenue area? Cab required at number fifty-six for a Mrs Smith. I repeat, cab for Smith, fifty-six Huntingdon Avenue.'

'I'm on it, mate.' Another male voice — a bit irritated, like someone who'd had a long day — crackled his reply. 'Where's the old dear going?'

Bill stood rooted to the spot. A glance at the girls showed they were at a loss what to do next. It was no point them bothering singing — their voices simply weren't being carried. Instead, someone was now booking a cab to the station at eight-fifteen the next morning.

From the audience came the sound of boos and whistling and the stamping of feet. One by one the girls stepped back from the microphones, frantically looking round for help.

They didn't have long to wait. Bill was nearly mown down by an entire posse of sound engineers shoving him to one side en route to the stage. And then the curtains came down and the audience erupted in fury at their entertainment being cut off before it had even properly got underway.

★ ★ ★

The sound of his phone ringing woke Bill from a deep sleep. At first he had no idea where he was. Then everything fell into place. The catfight. Prising apart a frantic Bea and a terrified Neela. Maggie appearing onstage in the middle of it, swearing like a trooper and ordering Bea to her room. Bea slinking off, Ginny skipping behind her to catch her up while the other girls glared after them, clearly shaken.

Reaching for his phone on the bedside table, he almost knocked it onto the floor.

'Pam?' His heart was thudding at a dangerous pace. 'It's four in the morning!'

'No, it's not. Not here, anyway. It's the middle of the day.'

Bill recognised her *no use arguing with me* tone, and took a metaphorical step back.

'How are you?' he asked. 'How was the flight?'

When there was no answer, he found

himself asking after Joely and the grand-children. There was a weighty silence coming from her end that he suspected bode ill for him.

'You're all over YouTube,' she said at last, having totally ignored his polite enquiries. 'You've had 27,000 hits. Little Ben found it. What were you doing watching *ChitChat*, anyway? You always have a go at me when I switch it on. Climbing over that woman and rugby-tackling those poor girls! What are you trying to prove, Bill?'

'Nothing,' he said. 'It's — well — this job I told you about.'

There was a long and protracted sigh from down the line. He missed her. That was the top and bottom of it.

'I was going to phone you after the show. But then there was a bit of an incident, and, well . . . '

'You got stuck in, and then you forgot.'

'I can't deny it,' he said.

A beat.

'Pam?'

'Yes, Bill?'

'I just want to say, well, that I'm sorry for everything.'

Always best to offer a blanket apology where Pam was concerned. Otherwise he'd find out he'd apologised for the wrong thing, and before you knew it they'd be back to square one again.

'Me too, Bill,' she said, much to Bill's surprise.

'Can we be friends then?'

Another beat. Then, 'Course we can, you daft thing.'

*   *   *

Once his conversation with Pam had ended, Bill found it impossible to sleep. He was in a quandary. Pam had decided to curtail her trip and would be coming home in three days. He longed to be there to greet her. But he was locked into a contract. What would happen if he broke it? Would Maggie Quinn take him to court and sue him for every penny he didn't have.

He thought he heard footsteps, and then a rustling outside his door. Oh, God! Speak of the devil! He certainly hoped not . . . but what if it was Maggie back to try her luck at seducing him? Well, he couldn't lie here cowering in his bed. He was going to have to put her straight. And, while he was at it, he might as well tackle the subject of his contract and get it out of the way.

Bill reached his door in one bound. His arrival coincided with the arrival of a folded sheet of paper sliding under his door. A note! He reached down and grabbed it. The message was simple.

We all did this stuff, it said cryptically. *But we're not bad. We're just frightened of Maggie.*

In a flash, Bill was out of the door without a thought for propriety. Ahead of him, a small figure darted away. Immediately, he was after her. She must have pressed the lift button, decided she couldn't wait, and legged it down the emergency stairs, because just as he reached it, the lift door slid smoothly open.

Bill jumped inside, thinking fast. Small girl, long hair. It had to be one of Bling-Bling. They had the penthouse suite. He pressed the button and the doors closed. When they opened, he jumped out, right into the path of a breathless Leila.

★ ★ ★

'The group's imploding now, so what does it matter about Maggie finding out what's been going on all this time?' Leila pleaded.

She'd dragged Bill with her to the suite of rooms she shared with her fellow band members. All of them had been in bed, asleep. But Leila had let the cat out of the bag, and was not about to waste any more time trying to shove it back inside.

'Yes, and whose fault is that?' Inez glared at Bea who glared back.

'It's all right for you, Inez,' Ginny chimed in. 'And you too, Neela. You've both got brilliant voices. And, Leila — you could have a career as a model that would earn you millions. But me and Bea . . . '

Bill looked from one to the other of the girls, trying to make sense of what they were saying. Were Bea and Ginny together the ones responsible for attempting to sabotage the group? 'Was it that, if you two couldn't have the glory, then no one else should be allowed to have it either?'

'No!'

Five pairs of eyes were fixed on him.

'Don't you see?' Leila said. 'We were *all* responsible.'

'If anybody's responsible, then it's Maggie Quinn,' Inez said, sharply.

It had been a long day, and Bill was exhausted. Couldn't one person please explain — and quickly — exactly what had been going on, so they could all get back to bed? When they all started up at once, Bill yelled for silence.

'Inez,' he said. 'What do you mean, that Maggie's responsible?'

'Because of her stupid contract,' she said. 'We signed it willingly enough, but none of us understood its implications. There's a thing called an advance. We've already spent it. But if we don't complete our quota of live gigs and promo work to support the three albums we've agreed to do, then somehow we're going to have to give it all back.'

'Add to that the fact that Maggie Quinn's influence in the music biz means she could blacken our names all over the industry if we pulled out, so we'd never get signed again. You see what we were up against?' This was from Neela.

Bill scratched his head. He was getting slow in his old age.

'No,' he said. 'I really don't'.'

Bea sighed heavily, contempt flitting across her face.

'Okay. Listen up. We thought we wanted to be in a pop band. But we didn't. Let's say it didn't suit our talents or our temperaments.'

He nodded.

'I'm a rocker, see. I hate the poppy music she makes us do. Ginny here thought she'd struck lucky when Maggie picked her for the group, because she thought it was the easiest way to land a footballer. Until she realised she had to work her butt off, which left her no time to find one,' she said. There was a mild protest from Ginny, which Bea waved away, almost good-naturedly. 'Inez fancies herself as a diva, Neela only really wants to play Nashville, and Leila — well, Leila got an offer from a modelling agency, which is all she ever really wanted, but she'd signed Maggie's contract by then, so she had to turn them down.'

Bill had never heard her say so much at once.

'You couldn't get out legitimately, so you attempted to sabotage yourselves.' Saying it aloud didn't make it sound any less bonkers.

'We thought she'd come to the conclusion that we weren't worth the hassle,' Inez said. 'But she was always one step ahead of us. Bringing you in to babysit us so she could keep the show on the road. Pretending things were just accidents. Making a PR event of the chilli incident.'

'Maggie hates to lose money,' Bill agreed. 'So what about the music going off last night in Newcastle? Was that your doing too?'

Bea jumped in. 'Are you kidding?' she exclaimed. 'That was nothing to do with us!'

When the music died on them, it had shown their voices up for what they really were. It was the start of the rift that had opened up between them and led to their arguing.

'That's when I decided to come and

see you,' Leila said. 'I was tired of all the fighting.'

'I'm glad you did,' Bill said.

'I decided that, actually, I didn't want to get out of my contract after all. I'd been kidding myself. There's no way I could make a go of it on my own. It was safer to stick with the band,' Bea said.

'Same here,' Ginny said. 'But Inez and Neela disagreed. They still wanted out.'

'Yeah,' Bea sneered. 'All that publicity's gone to their heads. Their egos have got in the way. There's such a thing as loyalty, isn't there, Ginny?'

'Come off it, you two,' Inez said. 'You'd have done the same if you'd had the voices.' She turned to Bill. 'Between us, Neela and I rewired the feed. We thought that, if we messed up, then it really would propel Maggie into sacking us. That all the trouble refunding ticket money, and us getting a reputation as an unreliable band, might finally tip her over the edge.'

Bill fixed his eyes on Inez.

'You girls!' he said. 'Why didn't you just get yourselves a good lawyer?'

They looked at him, and then at each

other. They'd clearly never thought of it till now.

★ ★ ★

Bill was on his way to the airport to meet Pam. Maggie had rolled over when he'd said he was heading home. Since he'd solved her little riddle, there was no longer any need for him to stay on, he'd said. She'd barely acknowledged his departure. Too busy thinking of ways to make as much money as she could from the legal wrangle that would no doubt ensue following Bling-Bling's tide of revelations.

He looked forward to reading the coverage in Pam's celebrity magazines during the coming months. It was a story that he felt sure would run and run.

Making Changes

Tania dreaded the record coming to an end, because then she'd have to open her mouth and speak. Sofie Summer — sitting opposite her in the cramped radio studio, headphones clamped to her ears — smiled, stuck up two thumbs, and mouthed, *You'll be fine*.

Tania attempted a smile in return, but it seemed to slide off her face. *Fine*, was it? Maybe for the likes of a professional who could shrug off a radio interview as 'just a little chat between us two' with no difficulty. Sofie Summer could probably do this job standing on her head. Stick her in a crackly white overall at the checkout at *Toiletry Treats*, where Tania was employed as Deputy Manager following her recent promotion, and it might be a whole other story, though. But not even that thought made Tania feel better.

'And that was 'Heroes' by David Bowie. Appropriate choice under the circumstances, since my guest today on *Sixty Minutes of Sofie* here on *Local Blend FM* is widow and mother of one, forty-five-year-old Tania Harkness, who herself has become quite a hero on the Keats Estate where she's lived for the past twenty-five years, ever since she transformed her run-down problem area into a safe, attractive place to live.'

'I'm really not a hero,' Tania protested squeakily. 'Everybody mucked in in the end. Everybody's *still* mucking in,' she added. 'It needs everyone to be vigilant to keep the situation on the estate from sliding back to how it was.'

'But *you* were the inspiration in the first place, weren't you, knocking on residents' doors with a plan of action?'

Tania was at a loss how to reply. The only reason she'd agreed to come on to the programme in the first place, after much coercion from her friends and neighbours, was to spread the message about how anybody could make changes to their environment, however bad things had become, simply by getting organised — just like them.

But Sofie seemed determined to make out that she, Tania, had performed some sort of miracle single-handedly. She'd just opened her mouth to say so when Sofie, who clearly couldn't bear even a nanosecond of silence, leapt in.

'But we're jumping ahead of ourselves here,' she said. 'Perhaps we should start at the beginning.'

Sitting there, Tania listened to Sofie's dramatic description of the estate as 'a series of high-rise blocks on the outskirts of this old university town of Borford, a place of rubbish-strewn courtyards where residents, under siege from hooded youths from other estates nearby, locked their doors at night because they were too afraid to go out.'

Tania reminded herself that in less than ten minutes now the whole ordeal would be over, and she'd be able to go home and take off these ridiculous shoes that no one was going to see anyway. Once she'd accepted this, she even started to enjoy herself. None of the questions were as taxing as she'd dreaded, and on the one occasion she glanced at the clock, she realised that time was very nearly up.

'So, what plans are afoot for the future, then, Tania?'

Tania told her about the mums-and-toddlers group that a couple of the new mothers were in the process of starting up. She described the leaflet they were working on with the council that she hoped would inspire residents of similar estates to change things for the better. And she was just about to launch into describing the committee's plans for the summer fete when Sofie cut her off.

'Tania, I could listen to you speak all day,' she cooed. 'But time's run out. We just have time for the phone-in.'

Tania was completely relaxed at last. Answering a few questions from ordinary folk like herself would be a breeze, she decided.

And so it was. To begin with. A couple of callers who lived on the estate wanted to know how to become volunteers. A lady called Irene said how much safer she felt now that security had been improved, and a teacher from the local comprehensive congratulated her for being so community-minded.

'And we have time for one more caller. Janine? Are you there?'

There was silence, then some throat-clearing. *Someone more nervous than me,* Tania mused, suddenly feeling like an old-timer.

'Hello Janine,' she said. 'Do you have a question for me?'

The voice came through at last. Muffled, barely audible.

'Not so much a question. More an observation.'

Sofie leaned forward. 'Go ahead, Janine. We're running very short of time.'

'It's this. You sound like a saint, Tania. Clearing up all that mess on the estate.'

'No-o, I'm really not,' Tania said.

'But you haven't done all that well with your own mess, have you?'

Tania froze. Who *was* this? She glanced across at Sofie and read panic in her eyes.

'That son of yours, I mean. Funny how you managed to close your eyes to everything *he* got up to, isn't it?'

Sofie's voice cut in: unnaturally bright, even for her.

'OK, I think that's all for today. Thanks for your calls, everyone,' she said, before turning to Tania. 'And, Tania Harkness, you've been a brilliant guest. I'm Sofie Summer, and this has been *Sixty Minutes of Sofie*. See you tomorrow, everyone, and goodnight.'

Tania stood up and struggled to locate the exit in the gloom. It was too small in here. There was no air. She had to get out. Before she burst into tears.

★ ★ ★

How she managed to get home, Tania had no idea. She thanked God that this interview hadn't gone out live. The last caller's words would simply disappear — or so Sofie's producer, who looked about twenty, had reassured her.

Yes, she'd been humiliated in front of people she didn't know. But, standing waiting for the Number 1 at the bus stop, she gave thanks that the interview hadn't gone out on TV. Here, she was just another slightly overweight middle-aged woman in a dark coat, indistinguishable from the rest, with only her blonde highlights hinting at former glory. Apart from her ridiculous shoes, perhaps.

It was a relief finally to be on the other side of the door of her flat. While she busied herself making a much-needed cup of strong tea, she tried her best to banish that final caller's words from her mind. But it was impossible.

Whoever it was that had said those things had hit a nerve. Her thoughts turned to her son Rob, from whom she'd been estranged these past two years. He'd been nothing but trouble for a long time. But, because she loved him, she'd turned a blind eye. She'd even made excuses for his repeated exclusions from school that had finally resulted in his expulsion, putting everything down to his father's unexpected early death from a short illness.

It was then that he'd changed — become part of a gang on the estate. Got his kicks from his numerous brushes with the law. Bragged that he was too clever for them. Well, maybe he had been. Not all his friends had been so clever, though; and if he'd stayed around, who knew how long it would have been before he'd have been caught breaking the law himself?

It was over a girl that he'd finally left. Kelly Brown, a quiet little thing — unlike her mother, Drina, who you could hear coming two miles off. He'd got Kelly pregnant, but refused to stand by her. That a son of hers could behave in such a cavalier fashion had shocked Tania. *Your father will be turning in his grave*, she'd said. A phrase that still came back to haunt her as being perhaps the most tactless and the cruellest thing any mother could utter to a fatherless boy.

Of course, he'd pretended not to be hurt by her remark. But she knew him far too well. He'd reacted the way he always did when he didn't like what someone said to him. He went on the offensive. Packed his things and left, and hadn't been in touch since.

Where he was now, she had no idea. She'd tried his mobile several times for the first couple of weeks after he'd gone, but it soon became obvious that he'd changed his number. He'd left in the month of November. She'd got her hopes up that he might come back at Christmas, so they could make it up between them. She'd put up a tree and ordered a turkey just in case. But no Rob. Not even a Christmas card.

Another Christmas had passed since then. She hadn't bothered with a tree this time, and had made do with beans on toast for her Christmas dinner. She'd spent the day drinking heavily while looking through all the old photos she had of Rob. What had happened to the cute baby, the little boy with the gap in his mouth where his two front teeth had been? The hangover had lasted two days, and she'd barely touched so much as a drop of wine since.

★   ★   ★

She'd sat and thought about what to do for hours. It was ten o'clock at night now — not exactly the right time to make a social call, but she couldn't wait till tomorrow to start looking for Rob. That woman who'd said those awful things about her had done her a favour, if she'd all but realised it. She'd brought something home to Tania that she'd never acknowledged till now.

All this driving herself to put things right on the estate had been her way of making up for her failure to fix things with Rob. And she'd succeeded, too! If she could turn round the Keats Estate, she could damn well turn round her relationship with her son. But first she had to find him.

Tania rang Kelly's doorbell, rehearsing what to say when she finally answered. Maybe she was mad to come here, but even if Kelly had no idea where Rob was now, it was quite possible she possessed some information about him. She was part of that crowd after all, even if only on the fringes.

It was a shock when Drina, not Kelly, answered the door. She was a tiny woman, all skin and bone with deep lines already appearing in her face: carved out, Tania imagined, from her many years as a serious smoker. She glared at Tania with hard, cold eyes, and Tania's heart sank, knowing she was wasting her time expecting any favours from Kelly's mum.

When Tania stammered out her question, after a long-winded apology for disturbing Drina at this time of night, the look of contempt on Drina's thin face struck Tania as only what she deserved. Drina was here looking after her daughter's child — Rob's child. And it was Saturday night. Party time down at the Dog and Duck, Drina's favourite haunt, where the two-for-one Happy Hour extended way beyond midnight and the music was loud and furious.

'You can be sure she has no idea where your son is,' Drina said. 'And if you ask me, it's good riddance to bad rubbish.'

'I know how you must feel about him,' Tania began. She was about to say she felt the same herself, but Drina was in no mood to be conciliatory. The trouble with Tania, she said, was that since she'd started her campaign, she'd got above herself.

'I hear you're on the radio now,' she said. 'Showing off about what you've achieved. Covering up your own mucky business, more like.'

Tania had heard enough. She turned away and hurried off back home. She'd been foolish to come here. When would she learn to think before she started her hare-brained schemes?

★　★　★

Some people complained if they had too much to do. Tania could occasionally be one of those people herself. This week, however, she was grateful she had so much on, what with getting to grips with her promotion on top of her usual commitments at the Tenants' Association.

It all conspired to distract her from trying to work out who this Janine was. There'd been a moment during her altercation with Drina when she'd wondered if she could have been the culprit. What she'd said to her at the door of Kelly's flat hadn't been a million miles removed from what this so-called Janine had said.

But hiding behind a pseudonym wasn't Drina's style. If Tania hadn't got as far out of earshot as quickly as she could on Saturday night, doubtless Drina would have found a few more choice insults to hurl her way. And if anybody had been passing and happened to hear them — well, Drina would have positively welcomed an audience.

Today was a Wednesday, and Tania's working day had finished earlier than usual. She'd come home, had tea, and tidied up the flat. Feeling too restless to stay inside, she decided to take advantage of the lighter evening to take a walk and check out that patch of waste ground that they'd spent yesterday's lively meeting discussing how to utilise.

There'd been a fifty-fifty split between a skate park for the kids, and a mini-allotment where some of the older, keener vegetable growers could pass on their skills to the next generation. Tania couldn't help wondering why they couldn't do both, but had kept quiet for fear of making a fool of herself. If she could get a good look at the plot they were talking about, maybe she'd have a better idea of the amount of land they were dealing with. How big was a skate park, anyway? All the things she was expected to know these days! Honestly, it was exhausting.

She'd been trudging through the hard mud, thinking about all this, barely noticing the litter and the dog dirt and the discarded bits of metal that once upon a time must have been somebody's kitchen appliances, when a combination of a flash of movement and the sound of voices stopped her in her tracks.

It was a couple: he was tall, she much shorter. From their slim silhouettes edged against the sky — now beginning to turn dark — Tania guessed them to be in their late teens, maybe, or perhaps early twenties. Feeling awkward at the prospect of disturbing someone's romantic tryst, she thought it best if she changed direction.

But curiosity stopped her and she turned back. She realised she recognised them both. The girl was none other than Kelly. Petite, like her mother, but with fewer angles, and with chestnut-brown hair that floated thick and silkily down her back: so very different from Drina's, which had been ruined by years of cheap home dyes and bad haircuts.

She knew the boy immediately. Jordan King, a low-life if ever one existed. Rob's nemesis. Could you blame another person for your son's weaknesses? Mothers had been doing so since the dawn of time when it came to their sons. More fool them, probably.

Of course, it was dreadful for Rob when Jim died. But he wasn't the only boy ever to have lost his father. And whereas some children stepped up and became the man or woman of the house, Rob's reaction had been very different. He'd grown sullen, rebellious, and so, so angry. Ripe for the plucking for the likes of Jordan King who surrounded himself with disaffected boys like Rob. Very soon, thanks to Jordan's influence, the future Tania had hoped for for her son had been consigned to dust. How could she not hate him?

What on earth was Kelly doing hanging round with someone like that? Did she invite him into her home? Had she introduced him to her son? *Rob's little* boy? The thought of that man having the same kind of influence on a child that he'd had on Rob sent a sudden rush of fury through her blood.

It wasn't the only emotion she felt, either. She'd never asked what Kelly had called the baby. Pride, tinged with shame for her son, had got in her way. But it didn't mean she never thought about him, or ever imagined becoming part of his life. This child was her flesh and blood just as much as he was Drina's. The thought of the likes of Jordan King shaping her grandson's morals was anathema to her.

She stood stock-still, afraid to move. If Jordan saw her it would be just like him to accuse her of being some kind of sex pervert, stalking couples in the wild to get her thrills. Nothing was beneath that creep.

'For God's sake, why don't the two of you just beggar off!' she muttered, paddling her feet, which were beginning to get cold as it grew darker.

The longer she stood there, silently praying for them to move on, the more it occurred to her that something wasn't quite right between the couple. Each time Jordan moved closer, Kelly, head hanging, stepped back, resisting his advances. As for Jordan — well, he may have been smiling but his smiles had a cruel, bullying edge.

What was he saying to her? Why didn't she answer? She could have walked away, but she didn't. It was as if Jason had some sort of hold over her. Not love, surely? Nobody in their right mind could fall in love with a creep like that, despite his slim body and his handsome face.

She was just remembering how important physical attraction was when you were young, and thinking how long ago it was that she'd been attracted to anyone that wasn't on a TV or cinema screen, when Jordan made a sudden lunge at Kelly, grabbed her by the wrist, and pulled her towards him. Kelly shrieked and tried to pull away, but Jordan, much the stronger, was having none of her rebellion.

Tania's reaction was immediate and with no thought for the consequences.

She dragged herself out from her hiding place and strode towards them.

'Oi!' she yelled. 'Leave that girl alone!'

The two of them turned their startled faces towards her. Kelly, a look of relief on her face, shook her hand away; and this time Jordan made no resistance, but simply let it drop, a guilty smile creeping over his face at being caught out behaving in such an unsavoury manner.

'Are you all right, Kelly?'

Kelly obviously recognised her. The girl shot a covert look at Jordan, rubbed her wrist furiously, and lowered her eyes.

'Yes,' she muttered.

'We were just messing, weren't we, Kells?' Jordan said.

Kelly, eyes still lowered, gave a listless nod.

'Well, it didn't look like that to me,' Tania said, standing her ground.

Jordan's smile was fading now. He turned to her, appraising her with his eyes.

'You're Rob's mum, aren't you?' he said. When she refused to reply, he added, 'Kelly here tells me you were round her place Saturday, knocking the door down, trying to find out if she had any idea where he was.'

So, they were close enough to share the details of their everyday lives, were they? Which rather answered her question. The foolish girl was in a relationship with Jordan.

'If she'd been there, she'd have put you straight,' he said. 'Her and Rob are history. Kelly's with me now.'

He stuck out his jaw as if to rebut any challenge Tania might make to this assertion. Then he drew Kelly towards him, folding her in an embrace. It was frightening how a man could switch from nasty to nice in seconds, Tania thought.

'But if you still want to know where he is, then maybe I could help you out.'

Tania froze. Her insides were in turmoil. She wanted to throw herself at him and drag the information out of him. But she kept her expression blank, giving him no hint at how easy it would be for him to toy with her.

'Mind you,' he said with a snigger, when he'd understood she wasn't going to press him, 'you'd probably be better off not knowing.'

★   ★   ★

Billy Togher, with his mane of red hair and face full of piercings, was a drifter, occasionally returning home to the Keats Estate like a bad penny before disappearing weeks, months, occasionally even just days, later. It all depended on how long it took him this time to antagonise the person he happened to be sponging off.

Tania remembered him as a little boy — constantly hyper despite being under-nourished, and desperate to please to the point of obsequiousness. She'd felt sorry for him, saddled with a mother like his, who sent him off to school with no breakfast and who didn't seem to care what he got up to as long as he was out from under her feet.

Back then, had she — perhaps ever so smugly — given thanks that she'd never have a son who'd end up such a loser? Not while she put warm clothes on his back or good food in his belly. How the Gods must be rubbing their hands in glee now, she thought, as she shouldered her way back through the three-deep throng at the counter of the neighbourhood McDonald's, clutching the tray of food she'd bought.

It hadn't taken long to piece together a picture of Billy's favourite haunts. A few judicious questions in the right places revealed his fondness for the slot machines in the mornings, followed by afternoons spent trying to cadge a drink at the Dog and Duck, and a game of snooker with anyone still prepared to give him the time of day.

Of course, she could have asked Jordan King outright where he hung out, when he'd taunted her with the news that Billy had shared a room with Rob in the homeless shelter. But that would have meant revealing how desperate she was to find her son, and she wouldn't have given him the satisfaction.

'It's so kind of you, Mrs Harkness.' Billy eyed the tray voraciously as Tania put it down on the table. 'Really, really kind. I always said you was sound.'

'You're welcome, Billy,' she said.

This habit he had of fawning on people was his way of protecting himself against abuse, she understood that. But all the same, she found it more irritating than flattering. Best thing was simply to treat it like a nervous tic and ignore it, she'd long ago decided.

'Tuck in. And if you're still hungry after that, I can go back and get you some apple pie.'

'Awesome!' Billy fell upon the food in a way that only a hungry man could.

'I saw Jordan King the other day,' she said casually, when Billy came up for air. 'Said you told him you'd seen Rob.'

'I like your Rob. He's a nice bloke. Always decent to me,' he replied, returning to his food and — it was blindingly obvious to Tania — sidestepping any further mention of Jordan King.

'We lost touch,' she said. 'And I'd like to find him again. I thought you could give me the name of the hostel where you both stayed.'

'What, me and Rob?'

'Yes. Jordan said you shared a room together.'

Billy peered at her over his burger. 'That's what I told Jordan,' he muttered. 'Only it's not true.'

'Oh?'

What on earth could he have meant? She watched him glance round the busy restaurant surreptitiously, before reaching into his jeans pocket and drawing something out.

'It's a business card,' he said, placing it down on the table, still covering it with his hand. 'Rob gave it me. He told me not to let anybody know where he was. But I don't think he could have meant you, Mrs H. You're his mum, after all.'

He pushed the card towards her.

It was stained and creased now — brown with yellow writing on it. *La Luca*, it said. *Italian cuisine*. There was an address, a website, a phone number. *Fiskwold, Norfolk* — a small resort she knew well from visits with Rob and his father, when they'd still been a family. She'd taken him on her own on the odd visit during the summer holidays after

Jim's death, too. But it had never been the same.

She didn't know what to think as she turned the card over in her hand. Why, she could get on the phone right now and ask to speak to Rob. Tell him she was sorry and she wanted him to come home. She could even pay him a visit. Did she have the nerve to turn up unannounced? What if he sent her packing? She couldn't bear to be rejected a second time.

'Remember what I said, Mrs H,' Billy hissed. 'Don't let slip where he is to anyone, just in case.'

She glanced up from the card into Billy's face.

'In case of what?' she said. 'Is Rob in some sort of trouble? Who with? With Jordan King? Is that it?'

'I've said enough,' he said. 'I just think it'd be best, that's all.'

He'd finished his food by now. What could she do to get him to stay and explain what was going on between Rob and Jordan King? Then she remembered the apple pie she'd promised him. But it seemed that Billy had had enough to eat already. Not only that, but he was already out of his seat, clearly anxious to leave. He wasn't going to give her more useful information, that much was clear.

'Look, I've got to go now,' he said. 'I just remembered I said I'd help Janine move her old carpet.'

Tania did a double take.

'*Janine*? Did you say *Janine*?'

Well, that was a name that certainly rang a bell. Closing her fist round the business card, Tania gripped it tightly.

'Yeah. She's my half-sister. You might know her. She lives in your block. Top floor.'

Yes, she remembered her now — long and skinny, just like her half-brother, but as far removed from any degree of affability as he was from surliness. She'd seen her at a few residents' association meetings, looking oddly out of place, always coming late and hanging round at the back. Wasn't she one of Jordan King's chums too?

Sometimes, when she caught a glimpse of her there, she imagined her running back to Jordan and filling him in on the latest plan that would make the lives of decent residents safer at the expense of lessening even further his opportunities to make some sort of profit. This meeting today had proved profitable for her in more ways than one.

'Well,' she said, getting up, 'I hope she's taking care of you and keeping you out of trouble. Be sure to give her my regards when you see her, won't you?'

Billy raised an arm in salute. And then he was gone, leaving Tania wondering what to do about both bombshells.

* * *

Tania wandered up and down the aisles putting the stock displays to rights. Since leaving Billy, she'd made a huge decision. She was going to write a letter to Rob. She noticed the two-for-one hair product display was a bit of a mess. She stopped to fix it, trying out phrases she might use as she did so.

I am very proud that you have managed to find work. No, that sounded patronising. Like she'd never thought he

88

was up to it. *I was thinking of revisiting Fiskwold when the weather gets warmer. It would be lovely to see you after all this time.* Too casual? Like they'd parted as friends and not as enemies? How about the truth? *Not a day goes by without me thinking of you. Do you ever think of me or have you forgotten all about me now?* Honest. But desperate. Dangerous, too. She'd know where she was if he answered that he never gave her a moment's thought. Or if he tore it up without even bothering to reply, which amounted to the same thing.

There was a tilted mirror fixed to the stand that reflected the aisle behind. Her attention was drawn to a solitary figure pushing a buggy slowly along its length, pausing every now and then to scrutinise the displays.

Tania recognised Kelly immediately, even though she wasn't looking anywhere near as glamorous as when she'd last seen her on the waste ground with Jordan. Today, her hair was scraped back, and she was wearing no make-up. In her outfit of jeans, trainers and hoody she was indistinguishable from any other girl on the estate.

There was something suspicious about the way her eyes kept darting about. Tania recognised it for what it was immediately — she'd seen enough shoplifters in her time to know that Kelly was on the rob.

And when the girl slipped a large bottle of high-end bath foam into the baby's buggy, Tania knew she wasn't mistaken. She'd moved off out of sight now, quickly towards the exit. Had she taken anything else besides this one item?

Tania stared after her, rooted to the spot. It was company policy to apprehend anyone leaving the store if you suspected them of taking goods without paying, and if those suspicions proved true then the police were called and a prosecution would follow.

So what was stopping her from going after the girl and looking inside her buggy for the stolen goods? A hot flush rose to her cheeks as the answer immediately hit her. Why, because alongside the goods she knew she'd find there, Rob's child was inside that buggy.

Her own grandchild — though she didn't even know his name. She couldn't get the police involved. What if they called Social Services and took the boy away from the estate? Though she'd never met him, she'd always held onto the hope that one day, maybe, she'd bump into him out and about with Kelly. But if he was taken away from his mother . . .

'You all right, Tania?' She felt someone's hand on her arm. It was one of the girls, Jamilla, who was gazing at her with concern. 'You look like you've seen a ghost.'

Tania shook herself. 'I'm fine,' she said. 'Miles away, as usual.'

'Thinking about that George Clooney film that was on last night, I bet,' she said with a grin.

'Yes, that's right.' Tania forced a laugh. 'How can I concentrate when I've got him on my mind?'

'Well, when you come down to earth, perhaps you can tell me if we've had any new deliveries of that anti-ageing face cream that keeps flying off the shelf?'

Tuesday was Tania's day off. She'd stayed up late the night before, composing her letter to Rob. By the time she finally went to bed, she'd lost count of the number of drafts she'd written before settling on the one that was now inside the stamped envelope inside her bag.

When she closed her eyes, she found she couldn't sleep. Words and phrases she'd written danced before her eyes, and several times she had to restrain herself from leaping out of bed, retrieving the letter and tearing it up.

There were other things too preying on her mind; Kelly, slipping the bubble bath into the toddler's buggy; Billy, giving away Janine's name. She couldn't let either of them go — the first was giving her a bad conscience, and the second made her itch to pay Janine a visit at the very next opportunity so she could scratch her eyes out.

Something else troubled her much more than either of these things, however. Billy had refused point blank to tell her why he'd lied to Jordan, or why she had to keep Rob's whereabouts a secret.

Jordan King's lean, handsome face flashed into her mind. Wherever there was trouble, he was always somewhere lurking in the background. He was like that cat in the poem they'd read at school all those years ago. Macavity the Mystery Cat: that was Jordan King, all right — sleek and sly and totally untrustworthy.

All this time she'd believed it was because of their dreadful row that Rob had left, when she'd told him that his father would be turning in his grave at the thought of his son evading his responsibilities to a pregnant girlfriend.

But maybe she was wrong and it was some other incident that had made Rob cut and run. Her last thought before she finally fell asleep was this — what exactly had Rob done to Jordan to convince him he'd be better off as far away from the Keats Estate as he could get?

And it was her first, too, when she woke suddenly, startled by the sound of someone hammering on her door. It was light — just about — though not light enough for her to be able to immediately locate her slippers. Tania sprang out of bed and groped for her dressing gown, finally finding her slippers by tripping up over them. She shuffled towards the door, which was firmly bolted. Things had got better on the Keats Estate, but you'd have to be a fool to leave your door unbolted before you went to bed at night. A fool to open it, too, without knowing who was on the other side.

'Tania. It's me. Mike.'

Groggy with sleep, Tania's brain refused to co-operate. The only person she knew called Mike was one of the committee members, who worked night shifts stacking shelves at one of the big out-of-town supermarkets. Why would he be knocking on her door at daybreak? It was with a feeling of trepidation that she slid open the bolt and opened the door.

'Can you get dressed quick, Tania, and come and have a look at the kiddies' playground? You're not going to like what you see.'

* ★ ★

Never had a truer word been spoken. Mike and Tania surveyed the scene before them with dismay. The children's playground had been completed less than six months ago. It had been intended for children no older than eleven, and for the mums, who enjoyed being able to take time out on the park's bright blue benches chatting to fellow parents as much as their kids enjoyed playing on the swings, slides and roundabouts.

Only now, the blue benches — like every other piece of equipment — had been graffitied over with heavy black paint. Worse — if there could be anything worse — the ground was littered with rubbish.

'It looks like someone's tipped the entire contents of their bin out, doesn't it?' Mike said, shaking his head in disbelief.

He had a point. At first glance, Tania could distinguish empty cans of lager and the various remains of several takeaways. Unwilling to take a closer look, she turned her attention to the graffiti. It was the usual mix of obscenities that no longer shocked, they were so commonplace. One thing was certain, though. The little ones wouldn't be able to play here until it had been cleaned up.

'More council money wasted putting this place to rights again,' Mike sighed, 'instead of spending it on all those other things this estate needs.'

'Did you see anybody, Mike? We might be able to get whoever did this.'

'Just a couple of lads. Three, maybe. The usual suspects. Wearing hoodies so I couldn't see their faces.' He paused, stroked his chin. 'Although, now I think of it . . . '

'Go on.'

'One of them had a face full of piercings. He made the mistake of turning round when I shouted for them to stop what they were doing. Ginger, now I come to think of it.'

Billy. Why would he do something like this? What was in it for him? Only yesterday in the restaurant he'd gone on at length about how much the estate had changed since he was last home, and how he wished it had been like this when he'd been a child, because perhaps if it had been then he wouldn't have got into so much trouble.

Tania had never felt so disheartened in a long while. It was as if she was back to square one, single-handedly fighting vandalism and with little hope of turning things around.

'I'll get some bin bags,' she said. 'Then we can make a start.'

'Not till I've called the police,' said Mike. 'Whoever did this won't get away with it.'

He seemed so certain. But for her part, she couldn't be so sure. If Billy *had* been involved in wrecking the kids' playground, had it been something he'd done when he was off his head on something? Even in that condition, wanton vandalism had never been his style. He had a reputation for many things — he was a sponger, and he was unreliable, and he was as flaky as they came. But if Tania could suggest one word that would sum him up the most accurately, that word would be 'victim'. If ever there was a man who could be preyed upon, that man was Billy. So who had preyed upon him to help commit such carnage in the early hours of the morning? And why?

* * *

Rob was happy here at the restaurant. He felt like he fitted in. Mostly that was to do with Tony, the chef — he'd taken him off washing dishes, which was what he'd been employed to do, and let him have a go at doing a bit of cooking, because he said he could see that Rob showed an interest.

Last week, he'd let him prep the starter and plate it up for a table of four. Said he'd done brilliantly. One of the regular sous-chefs had a habit of turning up late, and Tony wasn't very happy about that, understandably. Last night, when all the diners had gone home and there was only the two of them left, he'd said he was going to have a word with the boss about letting Darryl go and promoting Rob, in his place.

Rob had gone to sleep with a big smile on his face, and woken up with it too, once he'd remembered that he might not have to wash dishes for the rest of his life. But then the postman had stuck that letter from his mum through the door, and everything had changed.

It was a short letter, and the first time he read it, he'd taken none of it in. Truth was, he was shaking too much with fear. How had she got hold of this address? When Billy's name jumped out, he wanted to scream. He might have guessed. Never could keep his word, that one.

He read it again, this time taking a bit more in. Stuff about the estate and how hard she'd worked to turn it round. But that she was just fooling herself into thinking that was enough for her. *Come home, Rob,* she'd written at the end. *Let's start again.*

How much would he love to do that. Course he would. And to see his son, too. Then there was Kelly. But it wasn't that simple. How could he come home, knowing what would be waiting for him if he went anywhere near the estate? One sniff of his return, and he'd be dead meat. He wouldn't get as far as his mum's front door.

And how could he stay here now? He knew Billy of old. A couple of drinks, that was all it would take before he started boasting that he knew where Rob was living these days. He wasn't safe any longer. It was no distance to Fiskwold from Borford. For all he knew, Jordan King was on his way already, just waiting for an opportunity to get back what he insisted Rob owed him.

It was no use. Rob hitched his backpack up onto his shoulder and took one final glance round the room. If he valued his life, he was going to have to run away once again.

★　★　★

Tania was convinced, a couple of days later — when she turned up to clean the children's playground with the men from the council, armed with their industrial quantities of cleaning equipment — that only the usual suspects, her merry (if tiny) band of enthusiastic retirees, would be there to support her efforts.

But, to her surprise and delight, the

place was already milling with folk, wrapped up against the cold and eager to do their bit. Someone had brought along speakers, which lent a carnival atmosphere to the proceedings, and as the day wore on and more and more progress was made, it gladdened her heart to see how well the whole community were pulling together, just as she'd always hoped they would.

Tania — partly because she was determined to set a good example, and partly because the more she concentrated on the job in hand, the less she found herself with time to wonder about Rob's reaction to her letter, and when (or if) she might get a reply to it — probably worked harder than anyone else that day.

On the rare occasions when she got a moment to lift her head from her work, she scoured the knot of onlookers who'd collected to watch, rather than to participate, for any sign of Billy. She still couldn't get her head round the fact that he'd been seen running away from the playground.

There was no sign of him, but she did

spot Kelly, out with her mum and the baby, stopping to see what was going on before they went on their way. What with everything else going on with her life at the moment, the incident in the shop had slipped right to the bottom of Tania's priorities, and onto the list of things she'd rather hoped would go away. Sooner or later, she knew she was going to have to do something about confronting it — but now was not the time.

Round about three o'clock, helpers and onlookers alike began to drift away. Most of the playground had been transformed by this time anyway, and what was left could easily be tackled the next day, it was agreed. Along with everyone else, Tania helped load up the council van with the cleaning equipment they'd been loaned. She was mid-conversation with the driver when she caught a glimpse of Janine in the distance, her two little girls loitering behind her as they headed back home from the school run.

Seizing her chance, Tania set off in pursuit. If anyone might know where Billy could be found, then surely Janine would.

Janine was striding ahead, clearly a woman on a mission. The girls, however, were happy to dawdle, stopping at intervals to stroke cats, tie shoelaces, drop satchels, and pick fights with each other.

Tania soon caught up with them and passed them. Janine, who was now in touching distance, suddenly spun round.

'You two! Get a move on, will you!' she yelled. 'Oh. You,' she added, spotting Tania.

'Janine. Hang on. I'd like a word.'

Close up, the false tan, the painted talons and the hair extensions were overpowering. Her hair was jet black, all traces of her natural red covered up.

Janine sighed, reached in her pocket and withdrew a stick of chewing gum, which she unwrapped and popped into her mouth before screwing up the wrapper and dropping it at her feet. It made Tania's blood boil to see such a display of civic ignorance, particularly given how so many people had just spent their day.

'Is that what you teach them? Your girls? That it's okay to chuck your rubbish on the ground?'

'Oh, dear. *Sorry face*.' Janine drew an

upside-down smiley in the air.

Tania had intended tethering the topic of conversation to the subject of Billy and his whereabouts. The last thing she wanted was to reveal how much she'd been hurt by Janine's attempts — however futile — to discredit her on air. But the words were out before she could stop them.

'Why did you do it, Janine?' she snapped. 'What have I ever done to you to make you want to hurt me so much, bringing all that stuff up about Rob? You of all people should surely be able to show a bit of compassion.'

'What do you mean?'

'You know damn well what I mean! Ringing up the radio station like that.'

'Oh, that! It was just a joke,' she said, flippantly.

Yes, Tania could believe that. To people like Janine, everything was a joke. She'd be wasting her time even attempting to make some sort of connection with her. She should have listened to herself.

'I was talking to your Billy, before,' she said. 'He tells me he's sleeping on your floor.'

Janine made a moue of disgust.

'Where is he now, Janine? Only I'd quite like a word with him.'

'What about?'

'That's between him and me,' she said. 'Have you seen him recently?'

She shook her head. 'Not since yesterday. Can't say I'm bothered much, either.'

They'd reached the security door of the block of flats now. Janine fumbled in her bag for her keycard.

'You coming in here too?' she asked.

Tania nodded. She looked back at the girls. They'd fallen back again, their eyes glued to the ground, deep in concentration.

'What you looking at?' Janine called out, ramming the keycard into its slot.

'Blood.' The two girls spoke the word in unison, gleefully pointing to a trail of dark spots they must have been following for a while, and which neither Janine nor Tania had noticed. She noticed it now, though. In fact, she couldn't take her eyes off the trail that led straight to the entrance before disappearing somewhere inside. Tania didn't like the look of this one bit.

'What the . . . ' Janine squealed, as Tania pushed her aside and strode inside.

She heard him before she saw him, a faint moan coming from somewhere in the shadows. He was crouched in a corner, his head slumped into his chest. Hearing sounds, he raised his head. His face, bruised and bloody, drew gasps and cries from the little girls, who'd caught up with their mother and run inside.

'Billy!' Tania cried out. 'What on earth's happened to you?'

★ ★ ★

When forty minutes had gone by and Rob still hadn't put in an appearance, Tony, wondering what was keeping the lad, had climbed the back stairs to the tiny box-room Rob rented at the top of the restaurant. There was no answer when he knocked on the door. Was Rob still asleep?

Tony suppressed a twinge of disappointment in the boy he'd already started to see as his protégé — the lad with the neat knife skills and the superior palate, who only last night had been unable to contain his delight when Tony told him about his plans to train him up as a chef.

He knocked again, this time calling out Rob's name. Still no answer. Tony turned the handle in frustration. He'd assumed the door would be locked, but it gave under his hand. Immediately he saw that the bed had been stripped, and closer inspection revealed that nothing of Rob's belongings remained.

Nothing, that was, except a crumpled envelope bearing Rob's address, and a sheet of paper, written on on both sides, signed 'Mum'. Letters were private, everyone knew that. But this was an emergency. He needed to know where Rob was and what had made him pack his bag and leave so suddenly. Something told him this letter might give him a clue at least.

★ ★ ★

Fortunately the damage inflicted upon Billy was more superficial than it at first appeared. Tania hadn't thought twice about getting Billy right away from his half-sister and his nieces. It was clear from Janine's reaction that when it came to compassion, she'd been dealt a meagre portion. Billy looked a mess, and she wasn't having him in her flat bleeding all over her furniture and frightening her girls, end of.

Now, bedraggled Billy sat at Tania's kitchen table while she did her best to clean him up. At first he refused to answer her questions about who had done this and why. But then she suggested that in that case perhaps they ought to send for the police and let them do the interrogating.

'Not the police, Mrs H,' Billy pleaded, 'I beg you. You can't get them involved. It'll only end up worse for me if you do.'

'So tell me who did this to you,' she said.

He gave a long and heavy sigh, clearly conflicted about giving away the name of his attacker.

'Billy,' she said, a warning note in her voice. 'What did I say about calling the police?'

'All right, all right. It was Jordan King. He did it.'

Now, why hadn't that surprised her?

'Somebody told him they'd seen me talking to you at the burger place. He knew you wanted to find out where Rob was living nowadays — when Kelly couldn't help, you came looking for me, he said; which he was right about, as it happened, wasn't he?'

She nodded.

'He came after me then. Said I'd lied to him about knowing where Rob was, and that I'd better tell him because he had some unfinished business with him. Said he'd come after you if I didn't tell him. But I wouldn't. So he went round and did the kids' playground to get back at you,' he said. 'He wouldn't dare do anything personal to you. Not after what you've managed to do for the estate.'

So Jordan King thought she was off-limits. It was scant comfort.

'Jordan King was responsible for the damage to the children's playground?' Tania said.

'Not him personally. He's not daft. He

sent some kids to do it, didn't he?' Billy said.

'But you were seen running away. I thought you'd done it!'

Billy screwed up his brow. 'Me? No! I was trying to get them to stop. They grassed me up. Little beggars. That's when Jordan came after me and gave me this.'

'Billy, this unfinished business with Rob . . . Do you know about it?'

Billy looked uneasy. It was obvious to Tania that he did.

'It's a long story,' he said. 'And I only know bits of it.'

'Well, we've got all night. Oh, and don't even think that I'd let you back to stay at your sister's — even if she'd have you, which I very much doubt. You're staying here.'

★ ★ ★

Rob strolled along the beach, keeping to the sea wall, just in case. He'd spent the day wandering around, desperate to keep below the radar. Fiskwold was a small town. If Jordan King wanted to find him,

110

then he would, you could be sure of that. He would want his money — no doubt he'd want the interest on it too. Two years' worth.

It was getting dark now. The bunch of guys he'd seen doing repairs on the beach huts down past the pier had packed up and left five minutes ago. It was time to try the doors. Just in case. The wind was getting up and he was convinced he'd just felt a drop of rain on his face. He needed a place to stay tonight. Tomorrow would come soon enough, and then — well, then he'd have to think again.

He'd missed both the lunchtime service and the evening service too. He imagined Tony getting frantic — the number of missed calls on his phone was proof that he was still looking for him. He felt ashamed, truth be told. Tony had put all that faith in him and he'd let him down.

Couldn't tell him why, either. Tony was as straight as a die. How would he react if Tony told him about the little sideline he'd had as a drug dealer back on the Keats Estate, doing Jordan King's little errands for him? He'd disown him.

No use telling him he wasn't that boy any more. That he'd been weak back then, with no ambition other than to be like Jordan, the Big Man with the kind of money that talked. Except, of course, Jordan King, for all his swagger, was only one in a chain of command and not the Big Man at all.

The night he'd been set on as he'd made his way back from his last drop-off was the reason he'd had to run away. Till then, things had been going great guns. Kelly had told him about the baby. At first he'd not known what to think about the news — only because he hadn't been able to tell from her face whether she was happy or if she thought it was the worst thing that had ever happened to her. Turned out it was a bit of both.

'We can't stay here,' she'd said. 'I don't want my kid growing up on this estate thinking that selling drugs is his only option in life.'

'We'll leave,' he told her, there and then. 'We'll move on, the two of us, start afresh. Go somewhere we can make an honest living. Tonight. As soon as I've done this last drop-off. I'll collect my cut from Jordan and then that'll be it. No more business between us.'

But that was when his luck had run out. His own fault for thinking of the future when he should have had his eyes and ears about him, thinking of the present and how to get back to Jordan with the two grand he'd picked up in exchange for the drugs he'd offloaded.

Rob made his way on silent feet from hut to hut, trying each door. The fourth one he tried gave. He was in. He gave thanks to the careless builder whose mind had probably been on the foaming pint pot waiting for him at The Crown instead of on making sure he left his workplace secure. Then he slipped inside and locked the door behind him.

Two grand with interest. What would that amount to now after so long? He'd had no choice but to run away. Couldn't even ring Kelly and tell her why he'd had to go. It would have risked putting her in as much danger as he was himself. He'd written, or tried to, once or twice.

But she'd never replied. Perhaps she

never loved him after all. Perhaps she'd only stuck around with him back then because he had a bit of cash. He didn't think of Kelly much these days — what was the point when she'd obviously moved on? He thought of the little 'un, though. Wondered about him. Or her. Wondered all the time.

There was a kettle in the hut. Mugs, too, and all the paraphernalia for making tea. Rob couldn't believe his luck. He made himself a hot drink with the last of the evening light for guidance. Then he settled down on the mattress on the floor and waited for daybreak.

He must have fallen asleep, because he'd been warm just a moment ago and now he was stiff with cold. He was sure he was no longer alone. There was someone outside, striking a match, inhaling a cigarette, giving a cough. *Please God, no*, Rob prayed. *Not Jordan. Please don't let it be Jordan King.*

The door handle gave. Rob's heart was beating fast. Any minute now, he'd kick the door in. And that would just be the beginning.

'Rob! Rob, man. I know you're in there.'

He recognised the voice immediately. That Glaswegian accent was unmistakeable. Tony.

'Look, whatever's the matter, can we not go back to the restaurant and talk about it over a bacon sandwich and a glass of Scotch?' he said.

Rob was tired of running. He didn't want to run any more. And Tony's bacon sandwiches were legendary.

★ ★ ★

Kelly stared at the bottle of bubble bath on the coffee table in front of her. It was early and she hadn't expected a visit from Jordan today. She wished he'd have rung before coming round to her flat because she hadn't dolled herself up the way he liked.

She threw a nervous glance in her son's direction. Archie always looked adorable in her eyes, but seeing him through Jordan's fastidious gaze, crawling around the living room floor in his food-stained pyjamas, his face still covered in jam from breakfast, she could see he how anyone less emotionally connected than herself might be put off.

'I'm sorry,' she said. 'It was the best I could do. The place was half-empty. Anybody could have seen me at any time.'

She almost said what was on her mind — that in fact she was convinced Rob's mum had been following her with her eyes all the way round the shop, and it was this that had stopped her taking anything else. But you didn't bring up Rob or his family in Jordan's presence. Not if you didn't want to set him off.

'You want to take a lesson from Janine,' Jordan said, leaning forward and placing his hands on his knees. 'Two hundred and fifty quid's worth of stuff, she brought me last week.'

She noticed some grazing on Jordan's knuckles. She looked away, feeling slightly queasy at the thought of how they might have got like that. And ashamed of herself, too, for continuing to associate with a man she loathed.

What did he see in her? she asked

herself, not for the first time. There were plenty other girls he could have had for the taking, willing to run his little errands just so they could get in his good books. Janine, for instance. Why did he have to keep mithering her? Couldn't he see how much she disliked him? Or was that part of her attraction for him? That scent of fear and revulsion she was sure she must give off? Jordan liked a challenge, she knew.

'Anyway, I didn't come round here to talk about shopping.'

'Oh?'

He hitched up his hip and took a packet of cigarettes and a lighter from his jeans pocket.

'I'd rather you didn't smoke in here, Jordan,' she said, stiffly.

Jordan raised his eyebrows, like he thought she was just messing with him. Nobody told Jordan King what he could and could not do. Not even in their own place.

'The kid,' she said, with an apologetic glance at Archie. 'He has a bit of asthma . . . '

'Sure, sure. I get it.'

He put the cigarette and lighter back and turned his attention to Kelly. She stiffened as he leaned towards her, took a hank of her hair in his fingers, and began to twirl it round.

'You're a good mum to that kid, Kelly,' he said.

She kept her gaze fixed on her knees.

'Can't be easy for you, though. Money-wise.'

'We get by.'

'But wouldn't you like to do a bit more than *get by*?'

'I don't want to do any more stealing, Jordan.'

She was adamant about this. He couldn't make her. Could he?

Jordan released the lock of hair he'd been twisting. 'I wouldn't ask you, babe. Not if *that's* all you can come up with after a week.' He sneered at the bottle of bubble bath.

She should have felt relieved. But you could never relax with Jordan. Once he had you, you were his forever.

'There's something else you could do

for me, though. You wouldn't even have to leave your flat. And the money would be — well — phenomenal.'

Kelly's palms had grown damp. She felt sick. Not *that*. Surely he wasn't asking her to do *that*?

'No, Jordan. Not for any amount of money.'

'Easy!' He placed his hand on her knee. 'I wouldn't ask a girl like you to lower herself that way,' he said.

'So what it is you want me to do?'

This was how Jordan worked. You could refuse once. If he liked you enough, you could even refuse twice. Maybe. But three times? No. Never.

'It's the small matter of a gun. It needs a home for a couple of weeks,' he said. 'Can't hide it at mine. Police are always watching me these days. But *you* . . . well, they've got nothing on you, have they? So I hope you'll say yes.'

* * *

Tania woke up with a good feeling. This was the day — she was convinced — that

119

the postman would deliver a letter from Rob. But she should have known that something would come along to spoil her good mood, and she was right. Just as she was putting on her jacket to leave work to go out for lunch, an agitated Kevin came bustling into the staff room.

'I'm glad I've caught you, Tania,' he said, waving a printout frantically in her direction. 'I've just had this from the police. It's a warning about a gang of female shoplifters.'

Tania felt her face grow hot. 'Shoplifters?' she squeaked. 'A gang?'

'Well, that's the speculation from the CCTV they've picked up at certain points around the precinct. Young mums, from the look of things, pushing prams or buggies. We're going to have to keep our eyes open.'

Tania's head was a whirlwind of disparate thoughts. If the police were right, then Kelly hadn't been working alone. So if she was one of this gang, who was the gang master? Jordan King's face flashed before her.

She *hated* that man. He'd got away

with too many things for far too long while others ended up paying the price. What would happen when one of these girls got caught, as they surely would?

What were the chances of them grassing up Jordan King? Very little, if they wanted to go back to the estate and take up their lives where they'd left off. Jordan would make damn sure of that.

All this was spinning round her head as she set off towards the Memorial Gardens with her lunch. It was peaceful there, and peace was what she craved right now.

When she spotted Kelly further ahead in the middle of the lunchtime crowd, she set off in pursuit of her, without giving a thought to what she would do when she caught her up. In no time at all, Tania was on her heels.

'Kelly! A word!'

Kelly carried on walking as if she hadn't heard. But Tania wasn't so easily dissuaded. Lurching forward, she made a grab for Kelly's hood. When Kelly spun round to confront her attacker, she looked as if she had the weight of the world on her shoulders. Her eyes were heavy with lack of sleep, and a rash of spots marred her usually flawless complexion.

'What do you think you're doing!' she yelled. 'You've frightened Archie half to death!'

A loud wail emerged from inside the buggy. Tania registered angry fists and two chubby little legs encased in a blue quilted all-in-one kicking for all they were worth.

'I'm sorry,' she said. 'But I have to speak to you.'

'I could call the police,' Kelly went on. 'You damn well assaulted me.'

'The police! That's the last thing you'd do, Kelly!'

'What do you mean?' Kelly looked suddenly wary.

'I saw you. Stealing. The police are on to you. I know there are other girls involved. Is it Jordan King? Has he put you all up to this?'

She wasn't prepared for what happened next. Kelly's entire body seemed to collapse. Her face fell, and her eyes brimmed with tears that began to roll down her finely chiselled cheeks.

'Please,' she said, her voice hoarse. 'Just leave me alone. There's nothing you can do. There's nothing anybody can do about Jordan.'

She stumbled away, quickly picking up speed, and drawing looks of disapproval from other pedestrians as she pushed through the lunchtime crowd. Tania stood there, watching her until she disappeared completely from view. Well, she had her answer now. It was time to fight back.

* * *

Rob was back at work in the kitchen. The indolent sous-chef had been despatched and Rob had taken the man's place. He told Tony he felt bad about it, but Tony told him not to. In his kitchen, people had to prove themselves.

Rob got the message immediately. He'd never worked so hard in his life since Tony had dragged him back to the restaurant and put a chef's apron on him. But he loved it. He would have said he was happy again — were it not for the fact that he still hadn't written back to his mum, and more than a week had passed since he'd got her letter.

Tony burst into the kitchen, whistling tunelessly and carrying a tray of white fish on ice he'd just picked up from the supplier down by the pier.

'Look at that lovely lot,' he said, interrupting Rob's train of thought and slamming the tray hard onto one of the surfaces. 'I'm going to teach you how to prepare these beauties, so wash your hands and get yourself over here.'

Since working for Tony, he'd learned that speed was of the essence. Rob did as he was bid. The two of them worked companionably for some time, with Tony giving instructions and Rob concentrating hard to follow them to the letter.

'Written back to your mum yet?'

Tony's question coincided with Rob bringing down the knife, narrowly missing his finger. A minute or so went by before Rob replied.

'I've tried,' he said with a sigh. 'But I can't get the words right.'

'What about a phone call?'

'And say what?'

'Well, you could start off with *Hello, Mum, I got your letter, how are you?* I imagine that'd be enough to get the conversation rolling.'

'Yeah, and I also know what direction it would roll to, once we'd got the pleasantries out of the way,' Rob growled.

He held up a fillet to show Tony. Tony nodded. That meant he was pleased.

'I told you my story, Tony. I can't go back.'

'Because you're a wanted man, you mean?'

His sardonic tone wasn't lost on Rob. If Tony had been anybody else, he'd have slapped him with one of these fish heads.

'Look, Tony. This is serious. There's someone on that estate thinks I owe him two grand. He's not going to let it go.'

Rob turned back to his work, visibly bristling now.

'All I'm saying is, call your mum,' Tony said, gently. 'If you don't want to go *there*, ask her to come *here*. We can put her up for the night. Feed her. I'll put you in charge of the menu.'

Rob considered the prospect of his mother sitting at one of the tables in the splendid dining room in her best dress, sipping wine and admiring her surroundings, waiting with a mixture of anxiety and pride for her plate of food to be brought to her — cooked by her own son.

'Would you like that, Rob?'

'Yes,' Rob said. 'Yes, I would.'

'In that case,' said Tony, 'you'd better get on the phone and invite her.'

* * *

Billy excelled at keeping things from her. Fortunately Tania had neighbours who were less discreet. Several of them had helped him clear away the dog mess that had been dumped at the entrance to her flat the day she'd tried to reason with Kelly.

This had resulted in two things — the first was that Billy suddenly seemed to shoot up in people's estimation. He was suddenly the go-to person if a favour was required. If anybody was under the weather, he popped to the chemist for their prescription; he ran errands and walked dogs. He seemed to thrive on being given responsibility, and it gladdened Tania's heart.

The second thing that happened was that whenever anyone asked her what had happened to Billy's face, which was still full of cuts and bruises, she told them. When people began to draw their own conclusions about who was responsible for the vandalism in the children's playground and the dog dirt left on her doorstep, she didn't deny it.

One night, round about ten o'clock, Billy let himself into the flat looking rather shaken up.

'I've just seen Jordan,' he said, slumping down into a chair at the kitchen table. 'I had to wait in the shadows till he'd gone.'

Tania reached for the kettle. Billy looked like he needed a cup of tea.

'You shouldn't have to hide from the likes of Jordan King. No one should,' she said.

'I wish he was gone.' Billy gripped the edge of the table. 'Right away from here.'

The wave of sympathy she felt toward Billy suddenly collided with the tight ball of fury and hatred she felt towards Jordan, sending it spinning in a hundred different directions. She was so furious she almost missed what he said next.

'It was Kelly he was on his way to see.'

'What?'

'He sees her these days, doesn't he? And she lives over that way.'

Tania was already reaching for her coat. Right, that was it! She was sick of Jordan King terrorising innocent people. It was time she put a stop to his rule once and for all.

'You'll have to make your own tea, Billy,' she called out behind her. 'There's something I need to do.'

* * *

She heard the sound of Archie's crying even before she got to Kelly's door. Tania knocked hard, ignoring the irritating buzz of her phone coming from her jeans pocket. Billy, no doubt, worrying about her.

128

When there was no reply to her knocking, she tried again, even harder this time. Archie's wails were getting louder, and now it seemed as if Kelly had joined in too.

'Kelly! Open the door! It's me, Tania!' she yelled through the letterbox.

Drat that phone! She was about to give that damn Billy a piece of her mind when the door was flung open to reveal Kelly, with Archie hanging round her neck and screaming at full throttle into her shoulder.

'Not you again! Why can't you leave me alone?' a clearly distraught Kelly yelled through her sobs.

'Because you're clearly in a state,' Tania yelled back. 'And because Archie's sobbing his little heart out and somebody needs to do something about getting him to stop.'

Tania hadn't expected how she'd react if she ever got the chance to come so close to her grandson. The sight of him took her breath away. It was like looking at Rob as he'd been as a toddler. The same-shaped nose and mouth; the same eyes, full of curiosity. Strangely, at the sight of her, he stopped crying immediately, and the only sign that he'd ever been upset were the tears still glistening on his rosy cheeks. When he gave her a wobbly smile, she thought she might die of bliss.

Kelly however, as if to fill the space left by Archie's sudden silence, sobbed even harder. Archie, still gazing at Tania curiously, suddenly leaned away from his mother towards Tania and opened his arms. Without another thought, Tania took hold of him, revelling in his soft, warm embrace. She was over the threshold in moments.

'Go and sort yourself out, Kelly.' Tania took in the mess inside with one quick glance. 'Archie will be all right with me.'

But then her gaze faltered as — on the low coffee table in front of the settee all covered in toys — she caught sight of something. A shoebox, its lid lying next to it at an angle. Tucked inside the lid, unmistakeably, lay a handgun. Tania gasped.

'What the hell? Don't tell me that's

what I think it is,' she said.

Kelly's sobs had grown quieter, but now they reached a crescendo once more as she threw herself down onto the ground, crammed the weapon into the box, and clumsily replaced the lid.

'You saw what you saw,' Kelly sobbed. '*He* brought it. Jordan. He told me that if I keep it for one week, he's going to clear Rob's debt. So how can I possibly refuse? He'll go after Rob unless I do, I'm sure of it.'

Was Kelly really prepared to do this for Rob? Risk a prison sentence? For the second time that night, her phone started ringing. In a daze, she reached for it.

'Not now, Billy,' she whispered, without looking at the screen.

But it wasn't Billy.

'Mum. It's me. I got your letter.'

'Rob?' Tania fought against the sobs that were rising in her throat. 'You've got to come. Kelly's in trouble. She needs your help. We all do.'

★ ★ ★

One week. Jordan would be back to pick up the gun in exactly one week, because that was the night that something was going down, was what he had told Kelly. But they weren't going to wait a week for him to come round again, Tania had explained. There'd been a change of plan. He was to pay her a visit tonight.

Kelly made the phone call she'd been told to make. 'Jordan, do you fancy coming over? I've got a few beers in the fridge, and Archie's at my mum's.'

'Neither of these things are lies,' Tania had to remind her three times before Kelly plucked up the courage to make the call.

She'd taken Archie round to Drina's herself. Drina had needed very little persuading to get on board with Tania's plan, despite her previous animosity. What mother wanted to see her daughter put away for possession of a firearm? She'd got a couple of nieces to worry about, too. One of them she'd cornered and cross-examined about her shopping habits, and the girl had broken down and told her everything.

The other ... well, there'd been rumours about *her* for a few months now. What she was doing was much worse than shoplifting. Tania was right when she said the girl would never have chosen that lifestyle freely, which was why they needed to sort Jordan King out once and for all.

'All you need to do is open the door,' Tania reminded a nervous Kelly. 'Tell him you've changed your mind and give him the gun back.'

'Where will you be, again?' Kelly wanted to know.

Jordan was due any minute now.

'In the bedroom. You're not alone. Just make sure you get him inside with the door closed firmly behind him before you say a word.'

Tania heard him knocking on the door from her hiding place, quickly followed by Kelly's high heels click-clacking across the room. Chains rattled, the door opened. Kelly's voice was high-pitched. Would he pick up on her nerves? Then he spoke. *How about a kiss?* She imagined Kelly squirming, but she wouldn't refuse.

There was far too much at stake.

'I'll go and get the beer, shall I, then?' She raised her voice so everyone would hear.

Everyone who was hiding, that was. A couple of the men from the committee in the bathroom; two women members with her in the bedroom, who longed to give him a piece of their minds; and, in the kitchen, Rob and his boss Tony, the good-looking Scot from Glasgow who said he'd come along to give Rob a hand getting rid of the scum who'd put the mockers on him coming back home to see his mum and his baby son and his pretty girlfriend after so long.

'I don't know if she's still my girlfriend,' Rob had said at this, with a sidelong glance at Kelly. 'I left her high and dry after all, and I didn't try too hard to get in touch.'

'Because you were protecting me and Archie,' Kelly had replied; and he'd said yes, he was, but all the same he was sorry he'd not made more of an effort; and she'd said never mind, he was here now.

Yes, he was here now. *My son, Tania*

thought proudly, imagining him watchful and waiting for his cue. And here at last *was* his cue. She heard Kelly's heels again as she came out of the kitchen. If everything had gone to plan, she knew she'd be carrying not the beer she'd gone in for, but the gun.

'I can't do this, Jordan. You're going to have to take it back.'

Good girl. She'd done it. Tania held her breath. The silence seemed to last forever. But when it finally broke, it did so with a volley of words. Insults, threats, swearing — Jordan's usual limited display of language.

It was enough to bring Rob and Tony out of their hiding place. Tania heard the rush of feet. Instinctively, she pushed herself into the living room. She needed to see Jordan's face when they told him he was leaving and never coming back.

Jordan's shock at seeing the three of them — Rob, Tony and herself — slowed him down for a moment, but not for long. He launched himself at Rob, who took a step back, alarmed. He needn't have been, as Tony blocked Jordan before he could even land a punch.

'Take it,' Rob said, gesturing towards the weapon Kelly was holding out with both hands. She knew he was pretending to be brave for Kelly's sake. Perhaps, too, to show Tony that he wasn't going to have it all his own way. Men!

'You're all off your rockers,' Jordan said. He didn't know where to look now. At Kelly, or Tony or Rob or Tania. 'What's all this?' He was practically spinning like a top now as more people appeared from other rooms.

Everyone looked to Tania for support.

'You want to know what this is, Jordan?' she said. 'It's your official leaving do. We're tired of you here on this estate. We've decided we'd be better off without you.'

'You can't make me leave.'

'Oh, but we can,' she said, triumphantly. 'Take your weapon and go.'

★   ★   ★

It was Tony's night off. He wanted to see how his protégé performed from the other side of the kitchen, he'd told Tania. She thought it was a feeble excuse to ask her out to dinner, but she decided to humour him, telling him she thought this was a good idea. Rob might feel more confident without the older, more experienced chef breathing down his neck.

So far, Rob hadn't put a foot wrong, Tony had said, as the dessert arrived — a trio of tiny cheesecakes that looked to Tania like works of art, and tasted so delicious even Tony couldn't fault them. Not that he seemed in the mood to fault anything Rob had produced tonight. Tania couldn't imagine where Rob had got the idea that he was a slave-driving perfectionist.

'So,' he said, putting down his spoon. 'Jordan King's in custody.'

The police had been tipped off five minutes after he'd left Kelly's flat. When they'd caught up with him, he hadn't yet managed to lose the gun.

'Yes. So Rob's free to come home.' She took a mouthful of pudding, briefly losing herself in the flavour.

'Right enough,' Tony said. He returned

to his pudding; looking, she thought, disappointed.

'Of course,' she said, 'he's a grown man now, with responsibilities. A girlfriend and a son. And he seems to have found his feet here.'

Tony nodded brightly. 'There wouldn't be many opportunities for an up-and-coming young chef on your estate, I'm guessing,' he said.

'You'd be right. And he's learning such a lot from you,' she agreed.

'But wouldn't you miss him? Just when you've found him again?'

'I've got my own life, Tony,' she said. 'As long as Rob wants to see me now and then, and I can see my grandson . . . well, that'll suit me right enough.'

'So they're definitely back together? Him and Kelly?'

She nodded. It seemed very much so, she said. There was an awkward pause while Tony scraped the last bit of pudding from his plate.

'You get plenty of time off I hope?' he said, when he'd finished. 'Because — you know — he's not the only one who'd like to see you now and then.'

He glanced up from his empty plate, shyly.

'I'd like that too,' Tania said.

'That's if they can manage without you — at your job and on the estate, I mean.'

'I think they'll do very well,' she laughed. 'I'm not exactly Superwoman.'

'Oh, I don't know about that. Making your way as a widow and a single mum can't have been easy.'

The sight of Rob coming toward their table, dressed in his whites, a tentative smile on his face as he waited for the verdict, put a temporary end to their exchange. She gave him a thumbs-up, to show him he had no need to worry. She hoped he could read from her face just how proud she was of him.

Tony was right. It hadn't been easy. But she couldn't help thinking that from now on, her life was probably going to get quite a lot easier.

Another Country

We're having lunch on Mel's patio. The Californian breeze gently strokes my shoulders — which, unlike Mel's, are completely covered. Although I left Orkney forty years ago when I was just twenty years of age, I've never really been able to acclimatise to heat and strong sun. With my freckles and pale Orcadian skin, any protection less than Factor 50 and a burkha is suicidal.

My unwillingness to bare all during those years when a deep tan was something to strive for — even if it meant going through the pain of sunburn to achieve it — occasionally made me a curiosity. But I think maybe I'm having the last laugh now. Nowadays people — women, usually — comment on my English complexion. They sigh and point to the wrinkles they've accrued as punishment for their own reckless behaviour.

It's a nice compliment — sort of.

Except when we get to the bit about me being English. But if you live in the States and you come from a part of the British Isles that isn't actually England, you pretty much have to get used to that. The Irish have it easy. No one ever confuses their country with any other.

Today, like almost every day, the sky is a blinding, intense blue and there's no cloud to be seen. It goes on for mile after tedious mile, this blue, only interrupted by flashes of red-tiled roofs; scarlet, bobbing bougainvillea; and the stark green of palm trees that rustle in appreciation when they catch a breeze.

The pool is the same artificial blue as the sky. Paradise Villas, the condominium I've been calling home for the past two years, is a child's daub. The only hint of subtlety comes from the misty grey hills, so far away in the distance that they seem more like shadows of hills than hills themselves.

'But why, Shona?'

I allow Mel's question to hang in the air while I savour the last mouthful of the delicious fruit salad she — or, more likely,

Conchita, her Mexican maid — prepared earlier. Mel doesn't eat — she nibbles. Food, for her is a bore and a chore. She left the table some time ago, ordering me to 'finish up', an order I'm always more than willing to obey whenever I'm round at Mel's place. Conchita's lunches are legendary.

Right now Mel is stretched out on her sunbed, oiled up for some serious sun worship. She's too old to worry about skin cancer, she says; and anyway, a tan is slimming.

'Why exchange all this?' She stretches out her sandpaper-brown arms as if to embrace it all: the pool, the patio, the blue sky, her bracelets glinting and jangling in the sun, her manicured nails flashing red. 'For . . . what's it called again?'

'Hundsay.'

My island home has a population of one hundred and fifty. It perches on the edge of the ocean, so tiny you can walk it end to end in a day. In winter, it gets dark shortly after lunch and only gets light after breakfast. Sixty-mile-an-hour winds blow so hard they can knock a person over. For days on end on Hundsay, you can expect to be cut off from the mainland. This is how I've described to Mel the place where I was born and raised. No wonder she finds it difficult to grasp the fact that I've booked an open return leaving in November, of all months.

'Though did you say the men still wear kilts? I guess the place has one thing to offer, at least,' she jokes.

Then, more seriously, she asks if I even have friends over there anymore. It's been so long since I left that it's hard to imagine there'll be a soul on Hundsay I will recognise or who will remember me, I say. I don't add that not being recognised is exactly what I'm hoping.

'And where in God's name will you stay? Do they even have hotels over there?'

I try not to smile. In a place where the wearing of kilts isn't considered out of the ordinary, then Mel must think it entirely possible that the islanders dwell in caves, kill wild animals with spears and roast them on a spit.

'I've booked into a retreat,' I say. 'Skea

House. Used to be a private residence back in the day. Quite a prosperous farm. I thought it would be an experience.'

'Honey, it'll be that, all right. If you ask me, you must be crazy to think of going at that time of year.'

'Maybe I am.' I put on my sunniest smile, my way of saying the conversation is over. No use Mel trying to persuade me to change my mind. I've made a promise. And I can't break it.

* * *

The package had arrived two weeks previously to my lunch date with Mel. I didn't recognise the handwriting. From the stamps and the franking I could make out that it had come from Finland. Who did I know in Finland? Of course, my thoughts turned immediately to one person. Could it be him, after all these long years of silence?

I tore at the parcel, growing more and more frustrated at my inability to get anywhere with it. Whoever had sent it had made a damn good job of securing the contents. It took me five long minutes, a pair of scissors, and a broken nail to hack my way through.

Inside I found a small, square cardboard box and a letter. I decided to tackle the letter first. It was written in English — very neat, very correct — and signed *Jussi Karvonen*.

I skimmed the contents, each beat of my heart stumbling over the next as words and phrases pushed one another out of the way, fighting for my attention — *I am so sorry to write bad news . . . Mansie — there was nothing more the doctors could do.* My twin brother was dead.

I read it again. This time more slowly. This Jussi had been my brother's social worker, he wrote — a revelation I took in my stride. Of course my brother would have had a social worker. Either that or a probation officer. Actually, probably, even both.

But he felt he was more of a friend, the letter went on. They'd grown close, Mansie and him, particularly towards the end, when it became apparent that the tumour my brother had developed in his lungs was inoperable and the few people he counted as friends had stopped visiting.

The fact of Mansie's lung cancer didn't surprise me either. He'd been a smoker since boyhood. It calmed him, he used to say whenever I railed at him to give up; gave him something to do with his hands. Had it not been his lungs, it would have been his liver. Alcohol had always been another way he self-medicated. As for the friends who stopped visiting . . . well, that he had managed to amass any at all was a big surprise. To say Mansie didn't mix well was a colossal understatement.

He would have written himself, Jussi said, but writing was difficult for Mansie. He didn't have to tell me that. I'd known it all my life, right from when we first went to school and I would write my name at the top of my page then lean across his desk and write his given name, MAGNUS, for him.

I wrote his homework. I wrote his love letters. I wrote letters of apology on his behalf. In his early years, these were usually for broken windows and other minor transgressions; some accidental, some wilful according to my parents, pillars of the church but with little Christian spirit to sprinkle elsewhere.

But as he grew older, I progressed to writing letters of apology for the fights he got into, usually when he was drunk. They worked for a while, those letters. Till the day the Procurator Fiscal finally had enough of him and threw him in the cells overnight to consider his behaviour. Something poor Mansie was never very good at.

By now, my curiosity about the contents of the box was whetted and I tore it open, breaking another fingernail. The first thing that caught my eye was my silver ring. I recognised it immediately as the ring my parents had given me at my confirmation. I thought I'd lost it, but after a couple of weeks when I'd vaguely fretted about it, I hadn't given it another thought.

It touched me deeply to think that Mansie had kept it all these years to remind him of me. But it made me angry too. If I'd meant so much to him, why had he blocked all those attempts I'd made over the years to get back in touch?

There were three other things inside the box. A pebble, smooth and white and worn; a wing feather from one of the squabble of gulls driven inland, screeching and swirling, when bad weather comes to Hundsay; and a pressed flower: tiny, purple and rare. Relics of my brother's lost land. For a long time I held the items in my hand and simply stared at them, tears misting my eyes as I imagined Mansie doing the same. Quickly blinking them away, I returned to Jussi's letter. Here I found the answer to my question: why he had never replied to my letters.

Mansie wants you to know that he is very sorry for all the pain he may have caused you in the past and for ignoring the many attempts you made to reestablish contact, he wrote. *But he says it was better that way. He has had some dark years. All of them, he says, self-inflicted, though I myself am not so sure of that. Nobody, in my philosophy, is irredeemable.*

I liked this man. I was grateful to him for befriending my brother and seeing some good in him when everyone else — family, friends, community — had given him up. Whatever it was that made it so impossible for him to fit in, I still don't know. There were doctors, there were diagnoses. But every one seemed to contradict the last. In the end, it was more convenient to tell ourselves that Mansie was — well — just Mansie.

Of course, I was just as guilty as everyone else for giving up on him. You might say more so, considering our bond of twinship. Yes, I'd put out feelers some ten years after I moved to the States, when I already had two marriages behind me and was feeling sorry for myself.

It would have been good to have a shoulder to lean on in those dark days, to joke with my errant brother that he was no longer the only black sheep of the family. But then my life picked up again. Soon I had a new job. I moved to New Hampshire where I made another home and new friends.

My new friends were respectable, professional people. I told myself I would never be ashamed to introduce my brother to them. But the abrupt manner in which I called a halt to my search for him soon belied that particular confection of sweet, self-indulgent lies.

When I met Aaron, ten years ago after years of being alone, I knew I was taking on a sick man; and no, I didn't want to leave New Hampshire which was paradise and move to a condo in California. But he fell in love with me and I was lonely and marriage seemed a good idea on balance. He never knew to his dying day that I even had a brother. Mansie, Hundsay . . . all that was another time, another life. Another country, both figuratively and literally too.

But now that other country was calling me back. Mansie had had one last dying wish, Jussi wrote, which was to ask me to return all those items — except the ring, of course, which was rightfully mine — to Hundsay.

I'm not sure why he wanted them returned or what the significance of any of these items is, the letter ended. *Sometimes it seemed to me that Mansie had his own sort of logic no one else could ever hope to figure out. I offered to make the journey for him, but he was adamant it should be you.*

The final sentences came as a real shock. I had to read them several times over before they sank in, and even then I didn't know how much to believe them.

Mansie wants me to tell you that he is innocent, Jussi wrote. *He didn't set those fires. Neither deliberately nor by accident. And he wants you to prove that he didn't.*

★   ★   ★

I'm in Hundsay again. It's Midsummer Eve. The simmer dim. Close to midnight but still light. In a couple of hours, God will turn down a dimmer switch briefly — before he turns it back up again less than an hour later.

The oldies hate the long days. It plays havoc with their routines. It messes up their body clocks so they can't sleep. We love it, though, because we're young. We don't care about routines. If we're tired, we'll fall asleep anyway, wherever we are, whatever we're doing.

There must be a dozen or more of us round the campfire down on the beach. It's the best time of the day. We've been released for a few hours from our humdrum summer jobs, and we have nothing more pressing on our minds than fun and romance.

I'm sitting on the sand next to a boy named Guy, pressed into the curve of his body. He's given me his sweater to keep me warm. I'm not really cold and I'm sure he knows it. But this is not about a sweater, it's about him telling me that for now, at least, we're an item. So while everyone else larks about around us, we sit apart, a little island on our own, relishing the promise of a summer romance.

But then from nowhere a discordant note erupts, shattering the harmony of the night. People stop talking and turn their heads towards it. Through the gaps in the bonfire I can just about make out a group of boys — maybe half a dozen or so. It looks like some sort of disagreement has broken out. There's pushing and shoving but some restraining too. And in the middle of it all is Mansie. As I knew he would be.

'Oh, God.'

I attempt to get to my feet but Guy stops me.

'I thought he was on the mainland for the summer,' he says.

I'd thought the same. It was because he was away I could relax, do my own thing, stop looking over my shoulder waiting for the next bit of trouble I was going to have to get him out of.

'I should go to him,' I say, struggling to my feet.

'No. It's time you stopped protecting him. Maybe he'll learn not to be such a tosser once he's been given a good kicking,' Guy says.

He's right but I hate him for it. He follows me as I pick my way through the sand and pebbles and discarded beer cans in Mansie's direction. When he finally catches up with me, he takes hold of me, tells me he didn't mean anything. Says something about not letting my brother get between us. Then he takes me in his arms and we kiss.

By the time I come up for air, the fight — or altercation, or whatever it was — is over. The boys stand in a circle, everyone talking at once about Mansie and what an idiot he is and how he should be locked up — the usual stuff I've grown up hearing, that I should be able to shrug off, but still wounds.

Mansie himself is striding off, his tall, sturdy frame stiff with barely contained fury. Wherever he's going, it's obvious he doesn't want anyone to follow him. The party's suddenly over. Once again my brother has managed to ruin it.

★   ★   ★

The air hostess is bending over me, her teeth too white to be natural, her make-up a mask of scary perfection.

'You dropped your magazine, madam,' she tinkles. I recognise that tone. It's the way you speak to the elderly. I must look an absolute wreck. 'I'd hate for you to trip over it if you need to get up from your seat,' she says.

I blink and slowly begin to take in my surroundings. That pill I took was a powerful one. I must have been sleeping for hours. But I don't feel any better for it. Worse, in fact.

As I come to, my dream gradually recedes. But I can't stop myself fretting about it, reliving it, wishing things could have been different. If I'd followed him I'd have calmed him down, convinced him that those boys weren't worth it. Because they really weren't, that 'cool' gang made up of the boys who went to the private schools in Glasgow and Edinburgh, who only ever came back to the island for a couple of weeks in the summer before jetting off to some other much more glamorous destination. The Wisharts and the Fletts and the Muirs, those ancient, wealthy Orkney families with their profitable farms and their generous dollops of land.

I could have said to Mansie, *Come home with me*, and he'd have said, *What about that boy?* And I'd have said, *What boy?* And we'd have laughed and gone back home together, arm in arm. But that wasn't what happened.

It's been a long flight from San Diego to London and it's not over yet. I've done my best to while away the time, distracting myself with magazines and food and films and half-wondering about the pretty young woman sitting a few rows ahead of me in Business Class, who seems to be turning an awful lot of heads and demanding a great deal of attention from the staff.

I close my eyes again, wearily contemplating the rest of my journey. A ninety-minute flight to Aberdeen and then the overnight ferry to Kirkwall before the last leg of the journey — the shortest bit — the ferry trip to Hundsay.

Sleep drags me back down and I'm back in my bed in my childhood home. Something is troubling me, disturbing my rest. The acrid smell of smoke drifts its way towards me and now I can taste it.

I don't know what started the fire then, of course. Next day, along with the rest of the island, I'll begin to piece together various bits of information I get from other people.

How they think it started when a bale of straw caught fire; how it spread,

159

silently, invisibly, creeping through the undergrowth. Someone said a spark caught the roof of the main house at the farm while the Wishart family slept. That they got out just in the nick of time, and now it's a ruin.

Someone else said most of the livestock belonging to the Fletts had inhaled too much smoke to survive, and they'd had to be killed before they reached their prime weight. And that there was so much damage to the barns at Muir Farm that they would have to be pulled down. Jobs would be lost. The locals depended on these families for work.

And then there was the other rumour. That earlier that night, Mansie Hendrie had got into an altercation with Robbie Wishart and his friends. Something about a girl, someone said. Someone else said it was about money. Another person said it was about neither, but some damage Mansie had caused to Robbie's car.

But however muddled the cause of the bother between them, one thing was crystal clear. Mansie was nowhere to be found. Opinion was unanimous. He'd started the fire deliberately and now he'd fled.

★ ★ ★

The air hostess is bending over me again, this time informing me that we're about to begin our descent and she needs for me to fasten my safety belt. I sit up, my mouth dry. I need the loo but I know she won't let me out of my seat till we touch down.

I swallow hard and stick my fingers in my ears as the plane begins to drop. It's almost like I'm shutting off the voice in my head that's telling me I've made a terrible mistake coming back.

★ ★ ★

I need to prove that my brother is innocent. But where do I start? Perhaps a long walk might go some way to putting my jumbled thoughts in order. I find myself heading out towards Hurdal, the village where I was born — if you can call two rows of houses, a kirk and its

161

adjoining hall, the local shop, and a play park, a village.

From Skea House the distance to Hurdal is five miles. *Not far at all*, I tell myself optimistically as I wrap myself up in my down-filled coat and tie up my bootlaces. It's a bright morning, but I've failed to take the wind into account. Head down, I set off along the open road. As kids, on blustery mornings like these, we used to say that the birds would be walking today.

The memory of that old joke momentarily distracts me from my purpose. Digging my gloved hands deep into my pockets, I stride on determinedly and turn my thoughts to how a prosecuting lawyer would deal with the evidence. He might wonder, for instance, that if Mansie wasn't guilty, then why did he disappear so suddenly?

Then there was the fact that the fire brigade found three fires had been started at various points on the island within a very short time of each other. That couldn't have been an accident. Somebody must have done it deliberately.

But there's also a case for the defence. One, Mansie denied it. Two, running away from trouble doesn't make you guilty. It was always Mansie's first reaction. Three, it's not beyond the realm of possibility that, if there were three fires, then either one other person could have started all three, or three different people could have started the lot.

Already I'm beginning to think like a detective. My investigative thoughts have occupied my mind so deeply that I've already reached my destination without taking in anything of my surroundings. It's made me hungry too — thinking always does. I suddenly long for chocolate, so when I find myself standing outside the village store — which has been greatly extended from how I remember it — I push open the door and let myself inside.

'It's a blowy one this morning.'

I know that voice immediately. Suddenly I'm back forty years, sitting on the top deck of the bus on my way to school five miles away, peering out of the window and waving frantically at the girl who stands at the bus stop waiting for it to pull up so she can step on.

Her feet clatter up the stairs, and she plonks herself down next to me, her school skirt hoiked up ridiculously high to reveal her thighs, her face made up to the nines, and reeking of cheap perfume. And that's it. We both of us start talking, and we don't shut up from that moment until we get a warning in form time that we'll be separated unless we do.

Gunn. I used to envy her so much when we were younger — her confidence with boys, the way she never gave a damn about what anybody thought about her, those curves of hers.

Now she just looks ordinary. She's dressed in overalls and her hair is short and grey. Those curves I once envied have gone to fat, and everything's gone south. She's wearing a wedding ring. It digs deep into her flesh. Who did she marry in the end? She must have had a great many choices. Will she recognise me, I wonder, with my expensively coiffured hair and my elegant clothing? And from the work I've had done over the years that no self-respecting Californian woman of a certain age and income would ever deny herself?

'Gunn,' I say, my voice hoarse with trepidation. 'It's me.'

Her pleasant smile falters, her brow furrows. Finally, she knows me.

'Shona,' she breathes.

Gunn and I didn't part on the best of terms. I was a fool to think she'd welcome me with open arms. When she thought I was just another tourist, her expression was pure affability. Now, it's as if a wall has descended between us.

'How are you?' I'm formal. As distant as she herself as suddenly become.

'I'm well,' she says. 'And you?'

I tell her I'm staying at Skea House for a while. She raises her eyebrows. *That'll be a costing you a pretty penny* is what she's thinking.

'You didn't move away,' I say.

She shakes her head.

'My family's here,' she says. 'Why would I leave?'

I hear the criticism in her voice. I left my parents without a backward glance.

'Your mum and dad? Are they still living?' I affect a light tone.

'Dad died ten years ago,' she says.

'I'm sorry.'

She shrugs. 'Mum's still here, though. Still living in the old house.'

I loved Gunn's mum. She was everything a mum should be. Tolerant, warm, wise. And she baked the best broonie ever. I'm suddenly overwhelmed with nostalgia for the afternoons I spent in Gunn's kitchen, escaping the latest row between Mansie and my parents back at home.

'I'd love to pay her a visit. Say hello.'

'I don't think that's a good idea.'

Her face is closed to me. But I persevere. *I have a job to do*, I remind myself. Gunn can help me in my quest. She must still know everyone on Hundsay. I can't even remember the names of the boys and girls who were at the party that night, apart from a few. She could be my partner. Cagney to my Lacey. Or perhaps the other way round. I never could remember which was which.

'Gunn. Listen. It wasn't Mansie who

started the fire. That's why I've come back. To prove it.'

Even to me the words sound like something only a mad woman would say. That's how Gunn looks at me. Like I'm crazy.

'Oh! So you have evidence of that, do you?' she says, once she's taken in my words.

I tell her about the letter Jussi Karvonen had written in which he told me how Mansie gone to his death swearing he'd had nothing to do with the fires. My words falter in the face of her cold reception, but still I persist, stumbling over my dissertation till I've reached the end.

And then she says, 'He ran away, Shona.'

'That's no admission of guilt,' I say. 'Even the police said so.'

She makes a clicking sound with her teeth. 'The local police are idiots,' she says.

'You can help me, Gunn,' I plead. 'You were there. You can help me remember the names of everyone who was at the party that night besides me and you.

Perhaps one of them did it. And we can find them. Set the record straight.'

Her eyes are on me but she doesn't move. Her stillness unnerves me, sets me off gabbling even more crazily.

'Guy Railton was there, remember? Him and me had a thing for a while. The Wishart brothers and their girlfriends from England. Craig Muir and a couple of his friends I didn't know. Your cousin — what was his name? Were the Flett boys present that night? I think so, but I couldn't swear to it.'

Her cold eyes flicker over my face.

'Party? I don't remember any party,' she says. 'I remember the blaze, though; and my dad going in to help put it out; and the injury he sustained to his arm and hand that put him out of work for the rest of his life.'

Her words shut me up immediately.

'I'm sorry,' I say. 'I honestly didn't know about that.'

'There's a lot you don't know about. Not surprising, since you took the first opportunity to get out of Hundsay and you haven't been back since.'

She turns her head away. It's obvious the conversation's closed. I turn and leave without a backward glance. But my feet must have a memory of their own, because they appear to have carried me to the door of Mrs Reid, Gunn's mother's house. As I stand loitering at her gate, wondering how I got here, she opens the door and steps outside.

She's older, obviously. We all are. But she still looks strong and hale, with her rosy cheeks and her sturdy legs. She's wrapped up warm against the chill and she has a companion. A small, hairy dog with short legs who scampers towards me, barking enthusiastically, his tail wagging.

'Hold your wheesht, Peedie,' she says and calls him to heel.

He obeys immediately and she lowers herself slowly and painfully to pat him on the head.

'I should have got a bigger dog,' she says as she struggles to get up again.

She could always see the funny side, could Mrs Reid.

'You'll be looking for me?' she asks.

'It's Shona, Morven,' I say.

'I know it is,' she replies. 'I knew it as soon as I laid eyes on you. And I'm fair blide tae see thee.'

Her sweet words bring a tear to my eye and I blink them away. *Me too*, I say. I'm fair blide tae see thee.

'Come inside,' she says. 'Tell me what it is you've been crying about.'

When I put my hand to my face, it's wet with tears.

★   ★   ★

This is a much warmer welcome than I got from Gunn. There's a cat on my lap, a dog at my feet and a fire blazing in the grate. And here comes Morven with a huge mug of tea and — oh joy — the biggest piece of broonie I've ever seen.

'I see Daisy's taken a liking to you,' she says. 'Though if you don't want her to steal your cake, you'll put her down.'

When I do Daisy throws me an injured look and slinks off beneath the table. I take a bite of the broonie, rich with ginger and stickiness, and it feels like I've never strayed far from Morven's parlour.

'So. What's this all about, Shona?'

I tell her all about my meeting with Gunn. It's only when I'm halfway through my tale, complaining how harshly she'd treated me and how impossible it was going to be now to prove my brother's innocence if my one friend on Hundsay refused to help me, that I realise how still Morven has become and how white her face has gone. And then it strikes me. She hadn't known about Mansie's death until this minute, and it has come as a huge shock.

Realising how selfish I must sound, and desperate to make up for my insensitivity, I apologise profusely. Impulsively, I reach into my bag and draw out the package containing the treasures Mansie sent me.

'Here.' I press the envelope containing the purple primrose into her hand. 'If Mansie were here now, I'm sure he'd give you this for your collection.'

Morven blinks a tear away, sniffs, and stares at the envelope, bewildered. I open it for her and the purple primrose falls out and drops onto her lap.

'Do you still press wild flowers?' I ask

171

her. 'You had a lovely collection, as I remember.'

She picks it up and holds it in the palm of her hand, staring at it wondrously. Then her expression changes and she's no longer sad. Instead, she's grinning, shaking her head in disbelief.

'The little monkey!' She chuckles quietly. 'So that's where it went. I should have guessed.'

'What do you mean?'

But I'm only puzzled for a split second before the full significance of her reaction dawns on me. Mansie. Of course. He must have taken it. He was round here as often as I was. Never when Mr Reid was home, of course, and not if Gunn were present either if he could help it. She'd tease him mercilessly, and flirt with him too. Poor Mansie was terrified of girls like Gunn. He was terrified of girls, period.

'You know, your brother wasn't a bad lad, Shona. He was just wired differently from the rest of us. There was no malice in him. If he says he didn't start the fires, then I think it's time we all believed him.'

Suddenly it's as if the clouds have lifted

and the sun has touched me with a ray of
hope. I have an ally.

'You'll help me?'

'If I can, yes.'

* * *

I stayed at Morven's till three in the
afternoon. As the sun began to set, she
sent me on my way, just as she used to so
I would have plenty of time to get home
before it got dark.

We talked and talked. I told her about
my life. She told me about hers. When I
said how sorry I was to hear about Mr
Reid's arm, she merely sighed and said,
'Aye, well.' Perhaps she knew I never liked
him much because of the way he used to
speak to my brother.

She spoke about Gunn, too, and about
how the two of them didn't get on these
days, though she wouldn't specify the
reason. Gunn's name is Stout now, so I
learned. Her husband isn't from hereabouts, but from the mainland. In
Morven's eyes, that will cast him as a
foreigner. She gave the impression she

didn't think much of him. There had been no children.

And then the conversation turned to the items in Jussi Karvonen's package. Perhaps each item had some significance, Morven said; a suggestion I couldn't help think intriguing. Were they clues, perhaps? she said. I laughed, and said she was a better detective than I was because that hadn't even occurred to me.

'Why did Mansie turn up like that, out of the blue, that Midsummer Eve?' The question had been playing on my mind on and off all day, and finally I gave voice to it. 'It was the middle of the week. Mansie was working on the mainland for the summer, remember? I think it was a friend of my father's who got him the job. Mansie would never have dared cross him by missing a shift and failing to get back there for work the next day.'

Though in the end he did cross him, of course.

Morven tilted her head to one side. 'Erlend Shearer,' she said.

Morven Reid doesn't say much, but what she does say is always going to be to the point. That's how I remember her from when I was a girl, and nothing's changed. Her husband was silent, too. But his was a different silence — menacing, like you'd better watch your step if you knew what was good for you.

Erlend was a schoolfriend of my brother's — his only friend, actually. Like Mansie, he was an outsider, probably because he was slow at school and overweight, and there were those who said he didn't wash and therefore smelled. I never got close enough to find out, but if Mansie did and he'd got a whiff of him it obviously hadn't bothered him.

'He went with Mansie to work at the canning factory,' she reminded me. 'He still lives on Hundsay. Over Kirkbru way. Go and see him. They were close. He might be able to tell you why Mansie came back that night.'

So here I am in the churchyard in Kirkbru, where Erlend tends the graves on the same day every week; exactly as he's done for the last ten years, according to Morven, who knows where everyone is to be found at any given time of any given day, luckily for me.

It's a cold morning. The wind is coming from the north and the sky threatens rain. There are no trees on Hundsay, so all there is between me and the cold wild sea is my down coat and my determination to find out something that might help me prove my brother innocent.

'Do you think you can stop what you're doing for a minute, Erlend?'

I feel like a mother talking to a hyperactive child. I've been here ten minutes already, following him around while he moves stiffly from one headstone to the next, removing dead flowers and other debris and shovelling it all into his big black bin bag. Physically, he hasn't changed much, apart from having lost much of his hair. The extra fat he carries has kept his skin smooth; and if he smells, well, the wind's on my side.

When I introduced myself initially, it was clear he wasn't pleased to see me. At first I put it down to the fact that he thought I was somebody official who might be after him for something he'd done or had omitted to do.

But his manner hasn't changed, not even when I explain who I am and why I'm here. In fact, he seems to be growing more and more hostile with every passing minute.

'Mansie did it,' he says.

Three times he's said the same, after each question I've asked. 'Do you remember that summer, when the island caught fire?' *Mansie did it*. 'I bet you saw a lot of each other, you and Mansie, when you both went to work on the mainland?' *Mansie did it*. 'Do you remember if Mansie mentioned why he was coming home in the middle of a working week?' *Mansie did it*.

He speaks with a stubbornness there's no perforating. He won't look at me. Instead, his eyes — embedded in so much fat they've practically disappeared — slide away to fasten themselves elsewhere. And I know why. He's scared that if I capture his gaze, I will prise open whatever secret he's keeping from me.

Because if I've had any previous doubts about Mansie's innocence, I'm now one hundred per cent certain that *Mansie did it* is not the truth, but a mantra that Erlend has been coached in. Maybe he believed he would get through the rest of his life without having to repeat it. But he reckoned without me.

'I don't think Mansie did do it, Erlend.'

My voice is quiet, my tone level. The last thing I want to do is alarm him. I'm speaking to his back now. He's on his knees in front of someone's grave, trying to look busy, rearranging the pebbles that have come loose around the headstone.

'I don't want to talk to you,' he says. 'I'm busy, can't you see? You need to go away.'

'I thought Mansie was your friend, Erlend. Friends help each other, don't they?'

As soon as I speak again, I realise I've gone a step too far. A man of his age and carrying so much excess weight shouldn't be able to move so quickly, but rage can stir even the most unlikely person to combat.

Suddenly he's on his feet. He brings his face close to mine. His hands are up. Big fat fingers creep closer to my throat. I'm about to be murdered in a desolate churchyard thousands of miles away from home. I should be terrified, but all I can think of is that those old school chums of mine who used to complain about Erlend's body odour were right. It would be funny if it weren't so ridiculous.

What happens next occurs with such speed that I'm left gasping. Someone comes between us — male, as tall and lean as Erlend is short and obese. I catch a glimpse of sturdy boots and an impressive jacket — one of those Arctic multi-layered affairs with flaps and zips that if you dared wear under a Californian sky, you'd die of heat exhaustion within seconds. Rough hands pull me away, and then I find myself outside the danger zone. I strain my ears to catch harsh words spoken, but fail to understand what's said.

Erlend dusts himself down; he turns on his heels and tramps off into the distance. I'm left alone with my rescuer.

'It looks like I got here just at the right time.'

He speaks in an accent I don't recognise. Every syllable pronounced, the vowels long and stretched out, the consonants clipped.

'Jussi Karvonen,' he says, holding out his hand. 'I hoped I might bump into you.'

* * *

We're far away from the shelter of the churchyard now, down here on the beach. Waves, whipped by the wind, toss and tumble like sea creatures at play, sending up a fine mist of spray that glances off my cheeks as I stride along. White birds board the skulking grey clouds and ride them, skirling and screeching, high above our heads. I wouldn't wish to be anywhere else this morning. I just wish *he* wasn't here so I could enjoy it on my own.

Confident of the terrain, I was more than capable of keeping ahead of Jussi Karvonen for the entire length of the narrow track that leads down to the sea. But now we've reached the relative flat of the beach, I suspect it'll be no time before he catches me up.

I tug my coat further around my body and set my head and shoulders against the chill. Jussi's footsteps, long and measured and muffled by the wet sand, are gaining on me; so I stride out, determined to give him no quarter, deliberately ignoring the fact that he's calling out to me. Some of his words are swallowed up by the wind and the noisy cries of the gulls, but I get the gist. He wants to know what he's done to offend me and why I'm running away.

I guess he thinks he's my knight in shining armour and I should be grateful to him for coming along just at the right moment to rescue me from Erlend Shearer's grasp. Instead, I'm seething with resentment.

But I'm also short of breath now, and it's almost a relief when I feel Jussi's hand on my arm slowing me down. I have no excuse not to stop. Especially when he points out to sea to show me something.

'Look,' he says. 'Can you see them?'

At first, I can only make out the outline

of one or two, their heads bobbing comically up and down and their drooping whiskers lending them the venerable appearance of learned professors. But gradually another comes into view, and then another, until there are about half a dozen — enough seals to make up a family outing.

It's hard not to be charmed by such a sight. The two of us stand side by side, silently watching them for a long time. Finally, I break the silence, explaining to my new companion how hereabouts seals are known as 'selkies'. He listens intently, his expression growing more and more absorbed as I delve further into the folklore that surrounds them.

I tell him about how male selkies have a reputation for seeking out dissatisfied young wives — those married to fishermen out at sea, for example. And about how a selkie will shed its skin and take the form of a handsome young man in order to ensnare one of these young women for himself.

'Of course, it always ends badly,' I say, with the flippancy of a woman who has had a lot of experience in her life of falling for the wrong guy. 'All the selkie's after is a good time before he returns to the water. But he has no concept of the jealousy of the human heart. Nor does he understand the lengths we'll go to to prevent our heart's desire from leaving us.'

'So what do they do to stop him?' he wants to know.

'They steal his skin,' I reply. 'That way the selkie's forced to stay on dry land with his new wife and his new half-human, half-selkie children, poor thing.'

I catch him smiling at my story. But if he thinks there's been a thaw in our relationship, then he has another think coming. Though I guess it's only fair to explain exactly why I'm so annoyed with him.

'You know, you should have left me to it, up there with Erlend,' I say. 'Two more minutes and he'd have backed off. Given me the name of whoever it is who's telling him to lie about my brother.'

I explain how Erlend kept repeating *Mansie did it* every time I challenged him.

'I agree it sounds suspicious,' he says. 'But from where I was standing it looked like he was about to attack you.'

I insist that, whatever he thinks, I was never in the slightest danger from Erlend. I knew him of old, I reminded him.

'When we were at school, he was always being teased. Kids would compete with each other to be the one to finally send him over the edge,' I explain.

'That couldn't have been very nice for him,' he says.

'I'm sure it wasn't. But children can smell a victim, can't they?'

'Sadly, yes.'

'The thing is, Jussi, no one ever succeeded in getting completely under his skin. He always pulled back at the last moment, and either ran away crying or set about kicking whatever inanimate object happened to be lying within kicking range.'

'Maybe when he was a boy, he was no threat,' Jussi says. 'But he's a man now.'

'Yes. An unfit, overweight, *old* man!'

He nods, as if to give me the benefit of the doubt, still watching the seals, who seem to have lost interest in us now and begun to swim back out. I can see how he'd be good at his job. He's a listener and simply will not rise to any provocation. His passivity doesn't stop me continuing to want to annoy him, though. In fact it has the opposite effect.

How did he find me here anyway? I want to know. His answer is simple. He's been looking for me. He had an old phone number from Erlend's papers, and after a bit of detective work, managed to trace me from it to my home at the condominium where he got the number of Skea House through a phone call there.

'A pleasant, very chatty lady gave it me,' he says. 'You'd given her the key, she said. To water your house plants.'

That would be Mel. I'd have words to say to her next time we Skyped, about the definition of the phrase 'keeping a confidence'. It looks like I'm going to be having a similar conversation with the staff back at Skea House later today.

It was from a member of their staff he'd discovered where I'd be this morning, apparently. I wouldn't call myself the chatty type, but before I'd set off I'd asked if I could hire one of the bikes the retreat kept for the particular use of guests. I must have let slip I had an interest in the graveyard at Kirkbru. Obviously that's the kind of peculiar information that would stick in someone's head ready to be passed on to any third party who might be interested.

'So, why are you here?' I want to know. 'And how long do you intend staying?'

'I want to give you something,' he says. 'And then I'm leaving. Now I know you're serious about finding out who really caused those fires, there's no other reason for me to stay.'

★ ★ ★

It sits on the sideboard, next to Morven's a vase of expertly arranged dried flowers and a battered-looking photo album. It's in an anonymous square cardboard box. Morven and I have been standing in front of it since I arrived. It was my plan to tell her all about my conversation with

Erlend, and my intention — now Jussi Karvonen has left — to revisit him the next day so we can continue where we left off. Minus the strangling, hopefully. But then this happened, to drive everything else out of my head.

'I suppose we should open it,' she says.

Peedie — a sociable, curious little hound, who considers himself to be the third human being in the room — has left his basket where he'd been snoozing peacefully to see what all the fuss is about. If anything, he's more curious to find out what the box contains than I am. I already know what's in it. And I'm not sure how ready I am to come face to face with the contents.

'You do it,' I say.

'If you're sure.'

Morven's glasses have slid to the end of her nose. She peers at me over the top of them, her eyes small and bright. She's obviously had her hair done recently. The fashion for stiff curls for women of a certain age clearly hasn't changed in fifty years in these parts. A helmet of rigid grey curls stands guard over her soft round face. I feel a sudden urge to grab a hairbrush and brush them out.

'Go on.' I point to the scissors in her hand.

It's a matter of a few seconds for her to release the black urn from its trappings. A strip of white paper tucked down the side of the box says *Ashes of Magnus Graham*. At least that's what I assume it says. It's written in totally undecipherable Finnish and then again in Swedish which bears at least some resemblance to the English language.

'So, he came all this way to give you this, and now he's left?' Morven wants to know. 'Odd, don't you think?'

I give a little shrug, to show I have no opinion about that.

'Are you sure there was no other reason?'

I can't imagine what she's getting at.

'Is he good-looking?'

I roll my eyes. Finally the penny's dropped.

'Don't be ridiculous, Morven! At my time of life,' I reply.

'It's never too late for romance,' she teases.

'He said something about a conference in Edinburgh,' I say, choosing to ignore this remark.

Gingerly, I reach for the urn with both hands. I expect it to be heavier than it is. It's the sheer lack of weight I find so affecting. This handful of dust contained inside — is that all we come to in the end?

'What am I supposed to do with it, Morven?' I whisper, suddenly terrified.

I can feel my eyes brimming with tears. Funny, I thought I was over Mansie's death weeks ago. Even before I'd heard he was dead, I'd barely given him a thought in years. But now, holding the vessel that contains his ashes, it's almost like I've realised it for the first time. The urn may be light but it weighs me down with a mix of emotions. Sorrow for the passing of time; regret that I couldn't give my brother a happier life and guilt that I failed to make a bigger effort to save him from himself and from the world.

'I'll put the kettle on,' Morven says. 'And then we can discuss it.'

She makes her slow, stumbling way to

the kitchen. I have to quell my natural urge to call her back and to tell her to sit down and let me do it. Morven wouldn't take kindly to me drawing attention to her increasing frailty. Peedie wraps himself around her ankles in a way that terrifies me. How has he failed so far to trip her up and bring her crashing to the floor?

She's gone ages. I guess it's her way of giving me time to do my bit of grieving. I replace the urn in its box and set it back down on the sideboard between the dried flower arrangement and the photo album.

Curiosity gets the better of me. I pick the photo album up and take it over to a chair where I begin to leaf through the pages. I can hear Morven in the kitchen, clattering the tea things together while she chats to Peedie, who acknowledges her every remark with a short bark. It's an oddly comforting backdrop of sound that peels away the years and makes me think I'm seventeen again.

Initially, the photographs in the album are of stern-looking people from another century who stare at the camera in their Sunday best. A few pages on, and the black-and-white or sepia photographs graduate into colour, and people's poses become more natural.

Here's one of Morven as a young woman holding her baby in her arms — Gunn, of course. Gunn's father, whom I only ever dared address as Mr Reid, is featured too. Here he is as a young man, handsome in military uniform from the days when he was a regular in the British Army, before — according to Gunn — Morven put her foot down over his long absences. And here's another one of him, older, his cap at an angle, smoking his pipe, which is exactly how I remember him.

There are lots of Gunn, of course. School photos trace the journey of her physical development from the six-year-old with missing front teeth to the surly teenage years. In some of the pictures I recognise myself and Mansie as well as other local children, and linger over their faces for a long time, wondering what became of them all.

I've reached a page that features photographs taken at Gunn's wedding when Morven returns, carrying the tray, the ever-dutiful Peedie still coiled round her heels.

'Oh,' she says, when she sees what I'm looking at. 'Didn't I put that away?'

I go to shut the album, sensing Morven's displeasure at catching me poking around in her things without being invited. But then the page flips open again. There's Gunn, resplendent in her wedding dress, staring triumphantly into the camera lens, fully aware of how stunning she looks, her new husband a mere accessory by her side.

The picture below is of her alone. It's a close-up of the bouquet she's holding in her hands. An unusual shot, but no doubt taken to show off Morven's flower-arranging skills. Gunn's hands are cleverly arranged, too — in a way that shows off not just the bouquet but also the newly-acquired wedding ring on her left hand. Her right hand is in full view, too. And that's when I spot it.

'Peedie! For God's sake! Get out from under my feet!'

Morven's exasperated cry forces me to look up. I slam the book shut and jump up. Has Morven seen it too? A suspicious thought seizes me. Has she engineered this little accident as a way of distracting me from the photograph?

Peedie's scarpered, but not before he's managed to overturn the entire contents of the tray onto the carpet. I dash to the kitchen for a cloth and start mopping up, drowning Morven's apologies with a stream of nervous silly chatter of my own, until finally everything's been cleared up.

The damage isn't too bad. One broken cup, and a damp patch on the rug that Morven insists will leave no stain when it dries, so thoroughly have I attended to it.

This time I insist that Morven lets me make the tea. When I return, a guarded search with my eyes reveals that the photo album been tucked away completely out of sight. I'm convinced now that she's seen it too, on the second finger of Gunn's right hand. My confirmation ring. The one I thought I'd lost years ago, that Mansie returned to me along with the pebble, the dried flower and the bird's feather. I'd convinced myself he'd stolen it. But what if it was Gunn who was the thief — and all he did was get it back from her and return it to me, its rightful owner?

The conversation is stilted as we sit and drink our tea. Morven talks about the weather and how, if I were her, she wouldn't hang about too much longer. If it's a hint, I'm keen to take it. At the door, she tells me I must come again; but after what just happened, I can't be sure she truly means it.

'I just want to say, my dear,' she says, as I place the cardboard box containing the urn in the wicker bike basket, 'if you do go back and see Erlend again, please be discreet. He's harmless, I'll give you that. But there may be others behind him who could be less so.'

I think about her words as I ride off, but I'm soon distracted by open road ahead and the green meadows on either side of me. It's when I'm thinking just how misled people like Mel can be about this part of the world, and that they need to see how green it is for themselves because they'll never believe me telling them that it is, that I hear a sudden pop and realise I've got a puncture.

Skea Hall is a whole two miles away down a long lane at the next turning. I dismount, aware I have no choice but to walk the remaining distance. I've only been walking for five minutes when I hear a car approaching. It stops alongside me and a man steps out.

'Can I give you lift somewhere? It looks as if you might need one,' he says.

He's tall, with a pleasant local accent. When he comes fully into focus, I'm immediately plunged back in time more than thirty years. I'm looking into the face of Craig Muir.

'Let me put that in the boot,' he says. 'And I'll take you where you want to go.'

I can't speak for shock. Craig Muir would be my age, I realise. Could this be his son?

He extends his hand. 'I'm sorry,' he says. 'I didn't mean to alarm you. Gavin Charnley. I'm staying nearby. Can I give you that lift now?'

Charnley, then. Not Muir. But I'm certain I'm not imagining the likeness. It's there in the tilt of his chin and the slant of his cheekbones. There's nothing of Craig's calculating gaze or arrogant mouth, though — only a kindness in his eyes, and a smile that makes me say how very kind it is of him to offer. I watch him lift the bike and throw it with ease into the boot before I climb inside and fasten my seatbelt.

It's such a short distance by car that the drive's over almost before it's begun, so there's no time for more than minimal conversation. He knows I'm staying at Skea Hall, and he thinks he knows that I'm American. I've discovered he runs a business in Glasgow, and he's looking for a weekend place here on Hundsay to escape the hurly-burly of the city.

He drops me outside the main entrance, then walks round to the boot to get Morven's bike out. It's while he's handing it over and bidding me farewell that something tugs at my mind. Who else is it he reminds me of — this young, handsome man — besides a teenaged Craig Muir?

We wave goodbye to each other and I push the bike over to the covered stands while I ponder this new conundrum. Then I let myself inside and head towards the long curved staircase to my room.

The girl behind reception calls my name twice before I hear her. She asks me if I've had a nice day, and of course I say that I have. I can tell she wants more — everyone is so chatty hereabouts, I should have remembered, so I tell her about the puncture. It's not a problem, she says, they'll get it fixed, but she's sorry if it's caused me any inconvenience.

I'm about to make a joke about how actually, far from being inconvenienced, I was given a lift by a handsome young man. But before I can get the words out, his face floats into my mind and morphs with another face: a young Gunn. Could it be possible? Gunn and Craig Muir?

'Oh, before I forget. There's a letter arrived for you.'

The receptionist's words bring me back to the real word. I take it from her, noticing the lack of a stamp with interest. My name's scrawled on the envelope. My maiden name — Shona Graham. I wait till I'm in my room before I open it. The message is short and sweet.

Go home, it says. *You're not wanted here.*

* * *

The girl at the desk is surprised to see me this morning. As well she may be. I must look a total fright. I certainly feel it. My head is throbbing fit to burst thanks to last night.

I'm not a drinker. A gin and tonic at a party, a glass of wine occasionally. But yesterday evening there was a social event at Skea House — an opportunity for all the guests at the retreat to say more than a simple hello in passing.

It couldn't have come at a better moment for me. I've always been of the opinion that in any fight-or-flight situation, it's usually best to stay and slug it out. So I decided to take a hot bath, put on my glad rags, and make my way downstairs to join the party. Given the circumstances — the fact that someone seemed intent on driving me off the island — I think I ought to be excused for the way I hit the bottle: not so much Dutch courage as Scotch.

It was late when I got to bed, and I fell asleep immediately, still fully clothed. Two hours later, I was wide awake, and that ugly message was the first thing that came into my head. I remember staggering up off the bed, groping for the letter still on my bedside table, and tearing it into a hundred tiny little pieces before flushing it down the loo.

I didn't sleep much after that — there were too many things swirling round my mind. At the forefront was Morven. I needed to talk to her. She was keeping too many secrets from me, and I wasn't going to be able rest until I'd got to the bottom of them. First thing in the morning, I'd pay her a visit, no matter how hungover I was, I decided.

So now it's the morning and as much as I'd like to stay here under the covers and catch up on my lost sleep I have made myself a promise, which I must keep.

'It's a real mugga-fisty this day,' the receptionist remarks as, dressed for the weather, I pass by the desk on my way out. Her hands are full of loose papers, which she's attempting to put into some sort of order. 'That's what we say in these parts. It means . . . '

The severity of my hangover has played havoc with my manners. I cut her off before she can launch into an explanation of the term. As it happens, she doesn't need to explain to me what a mugga-fisty is. And to anyone who needed a translation, a quick glance through the window at the rain would say it all. *Wetting rain*, we call it in English. The kind that never stops from the moment you wake up till the moment you go to bed. Admittedly, 'wetting rain' doesn't have the same ring about it.

'That envelope you gave me yesterday. Tell me, did you see who delivered it?'

Her large, soft grey eyes look puzzled by what must appear to her a silly question. 'Wasn't it the postwoman?' she says.

There was no stamp on it, I tell her, so probably not.

'I'm sorry,' she says. 'I can't help you. It

had already been delivered when I started my shift.'

'So, who was on the desk before you?'

'That would have been Mairi.'

And when would Mairi be on duty again, I want to know. For a moment I'm optimistic. Mairi will be here any minute and I'll have my answer. But it turns out it's not my lucky day. Yesterday was Mairi's last shift before she went on holiday. For two weeks. To California. Oh, the irony.

'Is it important to know?' I've obviously stirred her curiosity.

'Not really,' I tell her nonchalantly. 'But if anything else arrives for me, perhaps you could take the name of the person who delivers it?'

She promises she won't forget, before returning to her task.

'And now I'm going out,' I say. 'Despite the mugga-fisty. Hangover,' I add, pointing to my head.

'I heard it was a good night,' she says.

'And a long one too,' I call out over my shoulder as I head outside.

I'm actually quite grateful for my hangover. It's put the brakes on my mind. Down here in first gear, I'm able to dwell on trivial incidents. Like the man I met at dinner, and our strange conversation. What was his name now? John? Jim? George? One of those instantly forgettable English names, anyway. He had an instantly forgettable face to match too — round and rosy-cheeked from too much alcohol, hair that was sparse and slicked back, the solid frame of a man who spends a lot of time in the open air.

It must have been round about my third whisky when I showed him the bird's feather Jussi Karvonen had sent me. I wouldn't have brought the subject up at all if he hadn't mentioned he was a keen birdwatcher, and how it was that hobby that brought him to Orkney as often as he could afford, now that he was retired.

Admittedly, had I stuck to water, I'd have probably refrained from waving the feather under his nose and saying, 'Full marks if you can tell me which bird this belongs to.'

To give him credit, he showed no surprise, only interest. It wasn't a gull's feather — he was adamant about that. After several moments studying it, he decided that it probably belonged to a bird of prey, though he couldn't be any more specific about which one.

But he hoped for my sake that I hadn't stolen it, or I might find myself in a lot of trouble with the law, he added. I think it was as he began to warm up about his subject, citing the RSPB and the Endangered Species Act, that I decided to slip away. I don't think he noticed.

Underneath my feet, the path to the main road has become a slurry. I didn't bring rubber boots with me from home, but alongside the supply of umbrellas and all the spare torches, the retreat has rubber boots in abundance. Or 'wellies', as I should probably remember to call them again, after all those years living in the States.

These ones are bright red. Not my first choice, admittedly, but they were the only ones that fitted me. What with these and my hat, which resembles a souwester, I must look like Paddington Bear. All I'm missing are the marmalade sandwiches.

I squelch along beneath the lowering sky, envisaging the scene ahead with Morven. How on earth am I going to play it? I have so many questions for her, but do I dare ask them? It's not that I'm frightened of her, but I hold her — have always held her — in great esteem. The last thing I want to do is accuse her of keeping things from me. Even if it's the truth.

I'm on the main road now. The air is tangy with salt. A pall of mist hangs over the sea, making it impossible to distinguish from the sky. Both are the same drab shade of grey. The wind is getting up but I refuse to allow it to deter me.

The weather changes quickly here on Orkney. *Four seasons in a day*, people joke. Unlike California, my adopted homeland, where the sun shines in a blue sky every day and the temperature rarely drops below sixty-eight Fahrenheit on a typical November day. I realise it's the first time I've thought about home since I got here. Do I even miss it at all?

★ ★ ★

I'm standing in front of Morven's house, trying to work up the nerve to walk up the path and knock on her door. The lights are on so I figure she must be home. Who wouldn't be on a day like today? I picture her in my mind's eye as I rap hard on the door. She'll have the fire built up and the cat on her lap. Peedie will be at her feet, of course. That loyal little chappy is never far away from his mistress.

After a couple of minutes, she still hasn't answered, but it doesn't worry me yet. She's slower on her feet these days than she cares to admit. Maybe she's even taking a nap. But when she doesn't answer after my third attempt, I start to wonder if something's up.

A glance through the front window reveals that in Morven's absence the cat is occupying her chair. She opens one eye when I rap on the glass, offering me a look of contempt before snuggling down to sleep again.

Of Peedie, there's no sign. He'd bark, surely, if he were inside? I tug open the side gate, slip round the back and peer through the kitchen window where everything looks as spick and span as it usually does. It occurs to me that the lamp in the front room may have been left on as a security precaution. It looks more and more likely that Morven has simply chosen to ignore the weather and gone about her routine as usual.

Damn! What am I to do now? I decide to give it five minutes and then I'll take myself back to Skea House. The rain's coming harder now, though, and the wind's getting up. I'm not sure if I fancy the return journey on foot.

I take out my phone. I know that if I make a quick call to the retreat, they'll send a car for me. I'm about to dial when I notice I've had a missed call from a number I don't recognise. How long has it been there? I wonder. I delay calling my answer phone till I've rung Skea House and booked my ride.

That done — I may have to wait up to an hour, I'm informed — I retrieve my message. It's Jussi Karvonen. 'I'm sorry I missed you. I'm still in Edinburgh. Can you call me back? I have some information — about Mansie — you need to hear it.' There's a pause, then, 'After dinner. Try at eight. I'll be free to talk properly then.'

I'm intrigued. What can it be? I wonder. It's a long time till seven, but I guess he's tied up at this conference all day. *Patience is a virtue*, I remind myself as I pick my way along the stony path to the bottom of Morven's back yard, as neat and tidy as her wee house.

I'm making for the shed, hoping she's left it unlocked and I can take shelter there. But when I try the handle of the door, it doesn't budge. For something to do, I wander round the back, where it's not so well-maintained.

The first thing that catches my eye, peeping up through the long grass, is a headstone splashed with red paint. Intrigued, I peer closer. It's not stone, but a piece of hardboard, cut out in the shape of a headstone, though admittedly one in a rather odd shape.

Scrawled on it in red paint are the words 'A bird that fell out of his nest and lived another 2 hours. No name. R.I.P.' Nestled at the foot of this little grave is a heap of pebbles. The number 2 is written the wrong way round, a mistake I find oddly moving.

It must be Gunn's doing, this touching little memorial. Perhaps some small tribute she'd undertaken as a sentimental child, though it's a side of her I'd never witnessed in all the years we grew up together. She was always so dismissive of nature, as I remember. This shrine to a dead bird seems so out of character.

Something — a flicker, a spark — begins to prickle my scalp. I feel I'm on the edge of making a discovery. If I can just keep still and concentrate, I'm certain something important will reveal itself to me.

But then I hear a dog barking and the flicker is snuffed out. It's Peedie. And here comes Morven, making her way slowly down her garden path towards me.

She's covered from head to foot in a voluminous cape so all that's visible of her are her two sturdy feet and the tip of her walking stick.

She asks me what I'm doing standing out here in the rain and wind, and insists I come inside and take a cup of tea, taking my arm and leading me back to the house.

Inside, while I'm removing my wellingtons and shaking off the rain from my gabardine, I half-listen to the story of her morning. She's had to take Peedie over to the vet's, she says, because she was worried he wasn't eating properly. Nothing to worry about, thankfully.

Personally, she suspects he's still living with the memory of breaking her favourite cup, and the upset has affected his appetite. He's a rare one, that wee dog, she says; lowering herself to pat him on his head. She's sorry she kept me hanging around outside; and in this dreadful weather, too, she adds.

'It's fine,' I say. 'I was admiring your garden.'

'You need to see it in the summer,' she

209

says, easing herself back up again. 'There's nothing much to see at this time of year.'

Now, would I like a cup of tea? she continues. Speaking for herself, she'd love one. She hobbles towards the kitchen. I could remain where I am, but I follow her. I'm not done yet.

'What's the story with the headstone?' I want to know.

I'm standing right behind her now. Her hand's on the kettle, waiting for it to come up to the boil. Two mugs stand ready and the milk's already in the jug.

I can't see her face, but I can read her back. Her shoulders have crept up to her ears and there's a long wait before she speaks.

'It's a long time ago,' she says, finally. 'Some nonsense of Gunn's, no doubt.'

I hesitate before I speak again. When I do, I hedge.

'Morven, I hope you don't mind my asking. But when I first came to see you, you mentioned that you and Gunn were no longer close. But you didn't say why.'

She turns round, a mug in her hand

that she holds out to me.

'It's complicated, my dear,' she says.

I've crossed the line. Totally blown it. I'm sure I have. If she refuses to answer *this* question, then there's no way I can bring up the subject of my ring on Gunn's finger, or the young man who gave me a lift who looked like a multi-mix of her and Craig Muir.

Orkney folk, I have to remind myself, are private people, not like those Californians I live with now who spill out their life stories on first introductions. I've known Morven a good many years. I like to think we're friends. Equals. But she's still a generation above me, I remind myself. Perhaps she feels the age gap is too large to make me privy to such personal family information. Or perhaps it's just too big to share with anyone at all.

A sharp rap on the front door puts an end to any further digging on my part. It's almost a relief when it turns out to be my ride. I drink my tea and kiss Morven quickly on each cheek before grabbing my wet-weather gear — too damp to climb back into — and heading outside, for the second day in a row relieved to be away from her.

I struggle against the wind, but finally I'm in the car, where I sink back into its comfortable warmth. Immediately, I close my eyes, and into my head pops the image of the shrine in Morven's back garden with its the oddly shaped head-stone, its childish red scrawl and the heap of pebbles at its foot. The number 2 written the wrong way round like that is the way Mansie used to do it, I remember fondly. How odd that I should think about that, after all these years.

In that instant, the flickering light I thought Peedie had extinguished with his barking snaps on again. Gunn wouldn't make a shrine like that. I'd thought so at the time, and I'm thinking it again now. But Mansie would.

It's dark now.

'We're in for a storm the night,' my driver says.

I mutter something back, to which he responds with a silent nod. I'm relieved we're done with small talk so quickly. I need this journey-time to think. In my hand, I'm holding the pebble Jussi sent me from Mansie. I roll it around in my hand. It's cold, smooth, and full of secrets.

What is he trying to tell me, my brother? First the flower, then my ring, and now this — the pebble. Three items, and all of them so far have led me back to Morven's house. Is it a coincidence? There's one more item — the bird's feather. Is that connected too?

* * *

Once I'm decanted from the car, the wind blows me inside Skea House. I'm so wrapped up in my thoughts that I fail to hear my name being called till I feel a tap on my shoulder when I've already reached the first landing of the stairs. It's the receptionist from this morning. I must come downstairs, she says. She's been going through the CCTV from yesterday, trying to find out whoever it was that delivered my letter.

'You've gone to a lot of trouble,' I say, following her back to the reception desk.

She's doing something fancy with her computer now that I don't understand. She tries to explain, but it's far too technical for me. I pretend to look interested, but what I'm really wondering about is who my messenger could have been.

'You looked so concerned that I felt I had to do something about it,' she says, her eyes fastened on the screen as she plays with the controls. 'Ah, here it is.'

At first, it's like an old speeded-up film, the kind we used to roar at with laughter at the cinema as children, but in colour rather than black-and-white. People walk backwards, hurrying in and out of the vestibule. Then suddenly the screen freezes.

'Right. Here it is. Look!'

She tilts the screen towards me so I can see more clearly.

'Wait a sec,' I say. 'I need my glasses.'

I scrabble in my bag for them. I'm all fingers and thumbs as I remove them from the case and pop them on my nose.

'Right, I'm ready,' I say, aware of how

breathy I sound and how hard my heart is beating.

Someone is walking through the main doors. They hesitate, as if wondering where to go next, perhaps even a little in awe of their surroundings. They glance this way and that before finally moving towards the reception desk.

Now they're at the desk, waiting to be dealt with. I can see it in their hand — the white envelope that contains that awful message. The receptionist looks up from whatever task she's doing, smiles, says a few words. She's obviously in a good mood — no doubt imagining herself far away on a sunny Californian beach, tanning herself. She holds out her hand and takes the envelope. Of course she'll see it gets put into the right hands, I imagine her saying.

Then the conversation is over, she goes back to her business, and the other person turns away and heads back the way they came. But for a second they look up, directly at the camera, and I see their face in close-up.

Though, actually, I didn't even need to

see her face. I knew who it was immediately she stepped over the threshold. That slow, ungainly walk; the old coat that's seen better days. Morven.

★ ★ ★

Whatever glimmer of daylight I woke up to has been snuffed out by rain that's progressed from a drizzle to one unremitting cascade of water. In addition, the wind has entered the ring and donned its boxing gloves. It looks like we're in for a rough night.

Talk at dinner is of the great storm of '53 when chunks of land were ripped away by floods, wind speeds reached 125 miles per hour, and roads were reduced to rubble.

Every now and then, the electric lights flicker. Round the table, we feign confident smiles. The staff reassure us as best they can. The walls are sound and the windows are triple-glazed, according to the waitress who brings our food, so there's no real cause for worry. It's the wee houses down in the town that are likely to be in more danger, they say.

Immediately I think of Morven and Gunn. Though why I should worry about what happens to them, since it's obvious neither cares much what happens to me, I can't imagine. *Old habits die hard*, I muse as I swirl my spoon around my soup.

Tonight's meal goes on forever, and for the first time since I've been here, I taste nothing. Finally it's over and I can get back to my room to make my phone call. Jussi Karvonen was quite certain he had something of great significance to tell me. Well, he's not the only one with a story.

*   *   *

The reception on my cell is poor. Jussi's voice keeps breaking up. I listen hard as he tells me that someone's been in touch with him — an old girlfriend of Mansie's, he says, who's contacted him to say she's remembered something Mansie once told her. Something that happened a couple of years before he left Hundsay in disgrace, he adds.

217

'She might have remembered it right. She might not,' Jussi says. 'You never can tell with Linda.'

'Because?'

There's a brief pause before Jussi replies with, 'She's an alcoholic. She occasionally has memory lapses.'

Already I've made up my mind that whatever this Linda has to say will be totally irrelevant. But when Jussi begins to tell me the story of the day that Mansie, out walking along the cliffs, came across a chick that appeared to have fallen from its nest, my ears prick up. Perhaps I'd been unfair to prejudge her.

'Mansie told her it was a special kind of bird — she couldn't say what kind. But rare, she said. He told her he picked it up, intending to carry it back home.'

Mansie loved all God's creatures. Probably because they're so uncomplicated. And, unlike human beings, they have no hidden agenda.

'Anyway, that was his intention,' Jussi continues. 'But someone intercepted him. A kind woman, she said. This woman saw how upset he was, and so she took him to her house, and . . . '

Morven. Of course. She would have helped him bury it in her back garden. She'd have helped him with the headstone, too. The inscription would have been Mansie's own creation, right down to the backward number 2.

That stealing eggs from endangered birds is a crime, I'm well aware of. You can make a fortune by passing them on to a collector. You can also — quite rightly — get put away for a long time for it.

It's hard to believe that Mansie was ever involved in that sort of thing. If anything, the opposite would have been more likely. He would have been the birds' protector, not their persecutor.

The line starts breaking up again.

'I wonder if Mansie was on the trail . . . Maybe they dropped . . . and Mansie . . . '

The line goes dead, but not before I'd already reached the same conclusion Jussi had reached. It's all starting to make sense. But who were the thieves? Not Morven — of that, I'm certain. Apart from the fact that she loved wildlife just as much as Mansie, there was no way she'd help my brother with one hand and deceive him with the other.

So, who is she protecting? Gunn? Admittedly, she stole my ring. But birds' eggs? Didn't you have to climb rocks to do that sort of thing? Gunn has never been that physically adventurous, as far as I remember.

My thoughts turn to Mr Reid, with all that army training he was forever bragging about. It had to be his good name Morven had been protecting all these years.

Just as I'm reminding myself of the old saying that blood is thicker than water, the light in my room gives a flicker of protest, and my surroundings are plunged into darkness.

★　★　★

The storm died down in the night. Now it's daylight, and the sun shines brightly in a clear blue sky. At some time during the early hours, power was restored. Now everything seems back to normal. And yet it's not. I have this new knowledge — or some part of it. Between them, Gunn and Morven must have the rest.

I attempt to commandeer a car to take me over to Hurdal, not fancying my chances on a bike this morning through the waterlogged lanes. There's a new girl on reception — holiday cover for Mairi, no doubt currently sunning herself on a Californian beach. Won't she be rubbing her hands in glee when she hears about the awful weather she's managed to avoid!

Her replacement looks at me like I'm some kind of crazy when I make my request. Can't it wait till things are back to normal? I'm saved from leaning across the desk, grabbing her by throat and yelling that actually, no, it can't, by someone hovering behind me.

It's not as bad as everyone's saying down Hurdal way, if that's where I want to go, the man says. He's just made a bakery delivery to Skea House, he adds, and now he's on his way to the village shop to do the same there. So if I'm ready to come with him straight away, he can drive me there, drop me near where I want to be, and then pick me up a couple of hours later to bring me back. I jump at the opportunity.

He can't know it, but he's playing right into my hands. Last time I breezed into the store, it had been a surprise to find Gunn behind the counter. Because I was so glad to see her, I had assumed the feeling would be mutual. Well, now I know the truth. She wants me off this island so I can stop meddling in her family's affairs.

This time I'm ready for her. When we get there — an easy trip just as my new friend Jimmy said it would be — the front door of the shop is wide open and Gunn hovers by the entry, sleeves rolled up, smoking a cigarette and looking cross. I guess she's been waiting for her delivery longer than she'd have liked.

I tell the driver I'll stay in the van for now, if it's okay with him, till he's got rid of his trays. I need to think about what I'm going to say. He's not curious. Just says that's fine, jumps down from the van, and walks round the back to get on with his job.

I pull my hat low over my face and turn

up my collar, like a '40s' sleuth, and sit and watch as he makes his way over to the shop with the first tray. The two of them exchange words, Gunn takes the tray, then he comes back for the second.

'She says her basement flooded,' the deliveryman tells me. 'She's only just finished mopping everything up.'

'At least it was nothing worse,' I reply, wishing he would just hurry up and get on with it.

He's soon back from his final trip. I jump out as soon as I see Gunn disappear back into the shop with the final tray. Then I push open the door. As soon as the shop bell pings, Gunn, who is busy arranging her wares, glances up. This time she registers who it is immediately.

'You still here?' she says.

'Yes,' I reply. 'I decided to ignore your message.'

'What message?'

She was always a good actor. You'd think she didn't have a clue what I was talking about, looking at her.

'The one you got your mother to deliver.'

'I don't know what you're talking about.'

Someone is coming down the stairs, their footsteps slow and heavy.

'I don't believe you.'

I'm angry with myself for tearing up the note. I want to flaunt it in her face as proof.

A shape appears on the other side of the bead curtain that divides the back of the shop from the front, and Morven pushes her way through. She's in her dressing gown — a fleecy, peach-coloured affair that softens her complexion and makes her look twenty years younger. She's holding Peedie in her arms.

'Gunn had nothing to do with that note, Shona,' she says.

I ask Morven what she's doing here, looking so very much at home. Hadn't she told me less than three days ago that she and her daughter didn't get on these days? It turns out that Gunn has a conscience after all. When she got news of the weather getting worse, she drove over and insisted Morven spent the night at hers.

'She's still my mother,' she says, defensively.

'Family ties are strong, aren't they, Gunn?'

There's a bitterness in my tone. I remind her why I came to Hundsay in the first place. She's not the only one with family ties.

'I have his ashes, Gunn,' I say. 'I know he would want them scattered here. But that can't be done until you tell me the truth about who started the fires that Midsummer Eve.'

She and her mother lock eyes. Morven is the first to speak.

'Shut the shop, Gunn,' she says, shifting Peedie from one side of her body to the other. 'I doubt you'll be getting many customers today. Shona deserves the truth, don't you think?'

* * *

The three of us sit round the table in the cramped stockroom at the back of the shop. Gunn has made us tea. She sets the mugs down in front of us, and when some of the tea spills over, she grabs a grimy cloth and mops it up.

'So what do you think you know?' Morven asks me.

'I think you're protecting Mr Reid,' I tell her. 'I think he was stealing eggs belonging to rare birds and Mansie caught him. Maybe he threatened Mansie — I don't know. But something frightened my brother enough to send him away from Hundsay forever.'

Morven widens her eyes. 'You're wide of the mark there, my dear. Jock was my husband, and we stayed together till his death. He stole those eggs . . . but it wasn't him I was protecting.'

She skewers Gunn with her fierce gaze. Gunn glances away immediately. When she speaks her voice trembles.

'She's protecting me. If it had just been Dad thieving eggs, she'd have shopped him right away,' she says. 'But she couldn't send me to prison. Not in the circumstances.'

I want to ask her what circumstances she's talking about, but I think I can guess.

'You admit then that you were responsible for stealing eggs?'

'No! I never stole anything,' Gunn objects.

I hold up my right hand and point to my confirmation ring.

'I saw you wearing this in your wedding photo, Gunn. So I'm not sure how you think you can get away with that one,' I say.

'Yes, Gunn. I'd like to know how you came by Shona's ring too. *And* how she got it back.'

'You don't know either?' I'm surprised that Morven's as much in the dark as me on this score.

'No,' she says. 'That's why I had that wedding album open, the day you came with Mansie's ashes. I couldn't help wondering where I'd seen it before. Of course, I'd seen it on your finger.'

'So, Gunn, go on. Tell us.'

It's a long story, she says. I remind her I've waited nearly thirty years already, so I can wait a little while longer.

It starts with Craig Muir, she says. She was in love with him. She thought he was in love with her. But she should have known that he was just stringing her along to save his own skin.

'Craig heard about a collector willing to part with a fortune for the right eggs. Skuas, plovers, divers; those kinds of birds. He thought it would be a laugh — something to do, you know?'

She shrugs, like she doesn't understand this attitude of his either.

'So how did you and your father get involved?'

Craig was clever, she explains, like I needed reminding. Clever enough never to get his hands dirty. That's where her father came in.

'He loved it. It was a military-style operation for him — abseiling into nesting sites, climbing rocks,' Gunn says. 'It was like he was back in the army. They went into partnership. He stole the eggs, Craig did the deals, and they split the proceeds fifty-fifty.'

But the trouble with her father, she says, was that he was careless. He must have left some evidence around the house one time, and Mansie spotted it on one of his many visits to see Morven. He must have grown suspicious, for he took to following Mr Reid to find out what he was up to. It was on one of these trips that Mansie disturbed him and he ran off, leaving Mansie with the dying chick.

'Craig found out about it from Dad,' Gunn said. 'He told me I had to stop Mansie going to the police.'

'Didn't you have any conscience that what they were doing was wrong?' I demand.

It wasn't that easy, Gunn said. Craig reminded her of the prison sentence her father would get when he was found out. And then there was the other thing. She was young and she was stupid.

'He cried. Swore he wouldn't survive in prison. Told me that he couldn't bear the thought of being away from me because he loved me so much. Like a fool, I believed him.'

It's an old story.

'You know, I had a reputation when I was younger for being easy. But it was always just an act with me. Craig was my first. We had sex one time and I fell pregnant.'

I almost feel sorry for her. But what she tells me next destroys every vestige of sympathy I was just beginning to feel. Of course, she did his bidding — went to see Mansie to plead with him not to go to the police. But Mansie was having none of it. What they'd done was wrong, and he intended to report it.

'So how did you get him to change his mind?'

Gunn looks away, shamefaced. It was wrong what she did next, she said. And not a day's gone by since without her wishing she hadn't. That was why she returned the ring to him via Erlend, after the fire, when she knew he would never be coming back. She didn't want to be blamed for something else he hadn't done.

'I went see him. Told him that if he breathed a word, I'd swear to the police that he'd raped me,' she said.

Morven lets out a horrified cry, which causes Peedie to give a yelp of sympathy.

'How could you do that to him, knowing how vulnerable he was?'

Right now I could kill her. Her tears

won't wash with me.

'I wanted to make Craig proud of me. Stupid, I know. I left, took a souvenir with me.' Turning to me she added, 'You were out, but you'd left your ring by the soap dish in the bathroom. I took it. To show Craig how cool I was.'

'Well, I hope you impressed him,' I said, bitterly.

Not as much as she'd hoped, she said. He insisted they still couldn't be sure Mansie wouldn't tell. That's why they lit the fires. She lit one, Craig lit the other. Her father was involved by that time. He initially thought starting a fire was a good idea if it meant getting Mansie off the island so they could stay in the clear. But when the flames started to spread, he realised it was all getting out of hand.

'He tried to put it out,' Gunn said. 'That's how he got his injury.'

I think I've heard enough now. I have to get out of here. But I have one or two final questions.

'Your baby. What did you have?'

'It was a boy,' Morven says, jumping in before Gunn can speak.

'Where is he now?'

'We had him adopted.'

'Do you still think of him?' I say, turning to Gunn.

Her answer will be very important.

'I look for him in every crowd,' she says.

I could speak now. Tell her I'm certain I've seen her son. But instead I say nothing. I get up, go over to Morven and give her a peck on the cheek. She's an old woman, and I still love her because she showed my brother love.

'You only wanted to protect your family,' I say.

'One day, I hope that you'll be able to forgive me for my part in this.'

She is stiff with grief and shame. She and Gunn have got a huge climb ahead of them. I'll be praying for them to make it.

★   ★   ★

I've never had children. But if I did have a child and I'd given them away I know I'd always be looking for them in a crowd too. We're walking along the strand, Jussi and I. He says he told me he'd be coming back to see me the night we spoke on the phone. That must have been about the time the line went dead.

Today the air is still — ideal for our task of dispersing Mansie's ashes. It's low tide and the sea offers no threat. At a distance a couple of contented seals bask on the skerry. The sun struggles to push its way through a watery sky.

Jussi is a very patient listener. His first response, when I wonder if I should have told Gunn I thought I'd seen her son, was that my lack of action was understandable.

'You didn't want to mislead her,' he says. 'After all you have no real proof the man you met was him.'

He's very kind. But very wrong. The truth is, I said nothing because I wanted to punish her. I still do. But I can't tell Jussi that. It matters to me that he has a good opinion of me.

'What if you're wrong and it's not him? It would be cruel to give her such false hope.'

I concede he has a point.

'But if it is, and what you say is true that he's looking for a house on Hundsay, then on an island as small as this it will be no time before the two of them run across each other.'

He's right. After all, didn't I walk into Gunn's shop?

He hands me the urn. With shaky hands I remove the lid.

'When are you going back to California?' he asks, breaking my train of sad thoughts about the brother I lost. I suspect he's trying to distract me and it's working.

'I don't think I will go back,' I say. 'It was my husband's county. I hated it.'

'You'll stay here?'

I shake my head. God, no, too many memories. You have to move forward in life. Even when you'll never see your sixtieth birthday again.

'I've always liked the idea of Vermont,' I say.

'Really?' His voice lifts. His eyes brighten. 'I have a brother lives out there. I keep meaning to pay him a visit.'

'Well, when you do and once I'm

settled there, you must be sure to pay me a visit too.'

I think we both know that we won't leave it so long. I walk slowly towards the water's edge. Once there I signal for Jussi to join me.

'Ready?' I ask him.

It's time to scatter my brother's ashes.

A MIDWIFE'S CHRISTMAS

Catriona McCuaig

Midwife Maudie and Detective Sergeant Dick Bryant are settling into parenthood, preparing for baby Charlie's first Christmas. But this December will prove to be one of the most eventful in memory. An unknown assailant is attacking multiple Father Christmases. A vulnerable young girl is missing, thrown out by her father in disgrace. And Dick's patience with Maudie's interference in police cases is wearing thin. Meanwhile, there are the politics of the village nativity play to contend with — from protecting soloists' fragile egos to wrangling live farmyard animals. Then a shocking event puts Charlie in danger . . .

THE SILVER CHARIOT KILLER

Richard A. Lupoff

It's Christmas week in New York, and the frozen body of Cletus Berry, Hobart Lindsey's partner, has been found in a back alley alongside that of a known criminal. Was there a connection between the two men? This wouldn't normally be Lindsey's case, but when a man's partner is killed, he must do something about it. Now separated from Marvia Plum, Lindsey is on his own, and the body count is set to rise unless he can solve the mystery of the Silver Chariot . . .

MALICE IN WONDERLAND

Rufus King

Three tales of mystery and the macabre. When the body of a woman clothed in the scantiest of swimsuits is found lying close to the surf on the private beach of a motel, Florida Police Chief Bill Duggan faces a baffling problem. Did she accidentally drown, or commit suicide? Or has she been murdered by one of the very strange guests at the motel? In other stories, a small girl's talent in witchcraft unmasks a killer, and a man's fourth marriage has a fatal ending.

THE RETURN OF THE OTHER MRS. WATSON

Michael Mallory

A new collection of puzzlers featuring the second wife of Dr. John H. Watson, of Sherlock Holmes fame. This time Amelia is plunged into a series of affairs that include the case of a carriage that vanishes into thin air, a jewellery theft on board an ocean liner, and an ancient royal document that may challenge the state of the sovereignty itself. As Amelia solves each case with resourcefulness and wit, she demonstrates the Holmesian adage: 'Once you eliminate the impossible, whatever remains, no matter how improbable, must be the truth.'